Father Christmas

Father Christmas
Spam the Cat's
First Christmas

BY

ELIZABETH ANN
SCARBOROUGH
WITH
K. B. DUNDEE

For Karen & Carl,

Meowy Catmas,

anie

Elizabeth Ann Scarborough

K. B. Dundee

Gypsy Shadow Publishing

Father Christmas
by
Elizabeth Ann Scarborough
with K.B. Dundee

Gypsy Shadow Publishing, Inc.
Lockhart, TX
www.gypsyshadow.com

eBook ISBN: 978-1-61950-27-3
First eBook Edition: January, 2012

Library of Congress Control Number: 2012933715
Print ISBN: 978-1-61950-052-5
Published in the United States of America
Manufactured in the United States of America

First Print Edition: February, 2012

Dedication

This story is dedicated to Kerry Greenwood and Karen Gillmore, whose encouragement has kept me writing and whose friendship made the holidays happy.

'Twas the night before Christmas and all through the house, not a creature was stirring; not even a mouse. Rats! While I'd been out chasing vampires and zombies, my furry housemates had hunted all the fun prey. Now my fourteen feline roomies were all asleep, our human mom Darcy was gone for the weekend leaving us on our own with just a cat-sitter coming in to feed us, and I felt restless. I was nine months old, and this was my first Christmas.

It felt like something ought to happen. It felt like something was *going* to happen, but I was pretty sure it wasn't going to be in my boring house with my boring friends and relatives.

On the other hand, it was snowing outside. We were having a white Christmas. Bah, humbug. Bad weather is what it is, the kind that clots white cold stuff in your paw pads. Unacceptable. I would wait until the weather humans came to their senses to go out, I had decided.

That was before I heard *the prancing and pawing of each little hoof*, apparently coming from up on my roof. I sat down to think, curling my tail around my front paws, my calm pose betrayed only by a slight flick at the creamy end of my plumy appendage. There *were* stockings hung by the propane stove with care, but a trip down that chimney would be disastrous for anybody, since they'd just end up inside the stove and wouldn't be able to get out. I considered waking my mother for a further explanation of the powers of Santa Claws. But then I thought that if anyone would know what was going on, it would be Rocky. I jumped onto the kitchen counter and stood against the corner cupboard. I am a very long cat,

1

even without taking my tail into account. My front feet could just reach the top cabinet, where Rocky liked to lurk during the day. Inserting my paw beneath the door's trim, I pushed. It smelled like vampire cat in there, but not as though the vampire cat was actually in there. Rocky was out. Well, it was night. He wouldn't mind the snow.

Some more scrabbling on the roof, and I suddenly thought, *what if Rocky has Santa Claws and is feeding on him?* He might. He was my friend, but he was definitely no respecter of age, gender, or mythological belief system.

I bolted out my private entrance. Only Rocky and I were able to come and go through that new cat flap that had been installed for me since my last adventure. I had a chip in my neck that activated it. Rocky had my old collar containing a similar chip, the one I'd worn before I went to the vet and got tagged.

The cold air hit me with a shock, and the snow wet my pink paw pads, though the heavy tufts of fur between them formed natural snowshoes. I was a very convenient breed of cat for this climate, actually. Maine Coon cats, or their undocumented relatives like me, were built for cold and wet and according to the Critter Channel, used to be ships' cats on Viking vessels. I didn't mind a nice trip around the bay on a nice day, but this snow stuff wasn't my cup of—well, snow.

I dashed into the snow without the benefit of any sort of vehicle, responding to the clatter, and from a safe distance, gazed back at the roof to see what was the matter. Other than snow.

The feel of the air shifted behind me, and I glanced back to see five deer step out of the moon shadows beneath the big apple tree. Nelda, Buck, and some other deer I knew fairly well—as well as a cat can know a family of deer, anyway—stood behind me, whuffing steam from their nostrils and looking up toward the noise.

I saw nothing special up there. Just weathered red tiles, our smokeless chimney, and snow falling on it.

"You guys weren't just up there, were you?" I asked Nelda.

"No, silly. How would deer get on your roof?" she asked.

"Well," I said, "You know—it's Christmas and everything, so I just wondered . . ."

"What's that got to do with Christmas?" Nelda asked.

"Oh, grandma," the young doe Gelda said, "Don't you know anything? Spam is under the impression that all deer are like those horned ones who pull that sled across the sky."

"What sled?"

"The one that's on half the lighted windows downtown."

Nelda shook her head, flipping off snowflakes melting on her muzzle. "Christmas is very confusing. I've been through several now and it never makes any sense to me at all. Why is there a sled with captive deer pulling it?"

"It's simple, Grandma," Gelda said. "The sled is magic, and the deer are pulling it through the sky, following a star that will show them where there is a manger with fresh hay. There are humans involved too, but that part isn't clear to me. The lights in the windows symbolize the star, I believe."

"Spam, that is species profiling, thinking we'd get up on your roof just because it's Christmas. Just because we live in this wet climate doesn't make us rain deer, dear," Buck said, snorting at his own pun. He's hilarious sometimes. Nelda and the other deer I've met are mostly as refined and classy as they look. I love deer. Most cats do, I think. They smell great and they are the prettiest creatures alive, other than cats. They have charisma—animal magnetism. It's a little lost on human gardeners; but we cats appreciate it, though Rocky says it's only because if we were a little larger, or they were a little smaller, we would find them tasty instead of merely tasteful. Okay, maybe they're a little hazy on some of the holiday mythology, but they are terrific critters.

Even Buck is handsome enough, if you like that sort of thing, and a lot of the does seemed to. But he was on the rowdy side and too big for me to be anything but wary of all that head tossing and prancing and showing off his antlers. Fortunately, he had respect for his mother, and she seemed to have decided to like me.

"You must have heard something too!" I said. I don't like being laughed at. "Otherwise, why were you looking up there?"

"There were strange noises," Nelda said. "And strange scents."

Just then, outlined against the snow, a masked face peeped up above the ridge of the roof.

"Renfrew?" I asked the coon. Who else would it be than my friend, sometimes assistant detective, and frequent moocher? "What are you doing up there?"

The coon opened his mouth to reply, then threw up his front paws, dropping something that clattered down the half of the roof facing me before sliding down the back. "Renfrew, wait!" I called, anxious to see what he was up to.

He didn't answer me, and I ran to the house to try to catch up with him, but he had slid off the roof and left a coon-shaped bare patch in the snow before waddling off toward the woods.

"Renfrew!"

"Merry Christmas!" he called back. In raccoon, of course, which sounded more like, "Iiiiiiiiiriii chirrittermaaaaw." But mostly, interspecies, we read thoughts for any real communication—sometimes you just can't say what you mean with barks, tweets, growls, or neighs—or other sounds. Meows, of course, and other cat language, are quite eloquent; but other species don't seem to be able to master the accent.

What had that silly coon been up to that he didn't even take time to stop and beg some kibble? What had he dropped? I thought he meant it was supposed to be my Christmas present. It was caught in the gutter. Double rats! Very inconvenient.

But I didn't want to miss out on a gift, so I raced around to the back of the house, where the scrap wood box was, and leaped up on it, thinking to mount the roof myself.

I jumped onto the steeply pitched part of the roof and slid much faster than I'd planned to down to the gutter, to the amusement of my deer audience. The snow had made the roof very slick, even with all my claws extended. I put a paw into the gutter, but it rattled and creaked alarmingly, so I pulled my paw back and tippy-toed along the edge until I spotted the gleam of silver and red.

Most cats would wonder why a raccoon would have a packet of batteries. I knew raccoons liked anything shiny. But in Renfrew's case, he might have wanted them for what they were made for, to power a phone or a radio or camera or something, at least until he decided to wash it. Renfrew was very clever with such things, which had come in handy when we were fighting vampires together.

It was really nice of him to give them to me, in that case, but other than batting them around the floor, I didn't have a lot of use for them. I'd just tell him this was the package I'd got for him for Christmas and give them back to him. No use wondering where they originally came from.

Biting down on the edge of the package, I jumped down from the roof. It's easier to get down than up. Carrying the battery packet in my mouth, I trotted to the edge of the driveway. The slight skim of snow seemed to have discouraged any cars that might normally be on the road this time of night. Understandable. It was pretty slick. Getting colder by the minute too. I cast one look back at my nice warm house. I could go back whenever I wanted to, have a nibble and a drink and settle down in my favorite office chair for a nap. Off to the right, the deer picked their way across the snowy brown grass, then paused. One of Nelda's legs hovered, suspended bent over the ground. Her head was up, watching the sky, or the stars, and Gelda and Buck followed her gaze. Then they moved on again, crossing the front yard of Bubba's house and on down the block.

Renfrew doesn't have a permanent address, being a raccoon of no fixed abode, as Bubba, the retired police dog next door would say, but he did have a general territory, though it was not his exclusively because there were too many raccoons around. He'd tried living under our house for a while, but said the upstairs neighbors were too noisy.

I didn't have to look hard for him though. A trail of packing peanuts and the noise led me to a tree near the one where we'd first met a couple of months before. Somebody was singing "Silent Night" with a lot of hissing and buzzing and an overlay of a football broadcast kicking in once in awhile that made the night anything but silent.

His den was a dump of more packing peanuts, torn up cardboard boxes, bubble wrap (ooh, fun to pop with your claws! I wondered if I could sneak a piece out of his stash and take it home to play with), and newspaper. Nestled among the packing stuff were various items that the Critter Channel does not usually mention when talking about raccoon habitat.

Renfrew did not look up. His paw hands were busy turning the noisy shiny white box over and over, looking for a way inside.

I dropped the batteries at his feet with relief. My teeth ached from clutching the plastic. "Here," I told him. "Merry Christmas. These are for you."

He could have said thank you. Instead he mumbled to himself—raccoons do a lot of mumbling and grumbling, I've learned—and kept fiddling with the box.

This gave me a chance to paw through the opened packages, sort of checking to see if there was one I might want to try on for size. A half-torn label was on the largest one, with an address, a Christmas sticker, and a UPS logo. Suspicion dawned.

"Where'd you get this?" I asked Renfrew.

"Found it," he said, finally looking up with big masked bright eyes full of innocence and wonder.

"Found it where?" I asked.

"Just laying around," he said. "There's all sorts of stuff just laying around right now, Spam. You wouldn't believe the things people put in these boxes and leave on their porches. I've noticed a lot more of them lately, so I brought some back to see if there was anything inside. There's been food in some of them. Here—" he reached a paw back and picked up a piece of something dense and colorful. "Do cats like fruitcake? Didn't care for it myself."

"Renfrew, I hate to tell you this, but they don't leave those boxes laying around for coons to find. They're calling you the UPS bandit!"

"I've been called worse," he said, dropping the fruitcake and flinging the white box aside in disgust before tearing into another, unopened package.

"You're taking peoples' Christmas presents!" I told him.

"They put them outside, Spam. Honest. They didn't want them."

"They didn't put them outside. The delivery guys brought them to the houses and left them outside for people to pick up when they came home. Except you got there first. There's more of them now because people are ordering Christmas presents delivered."

I put a claw through the plastic covering the box with a lady doll in a fancy dress inside. "This is some little kid's dolly."

He gave it a glance then went back to rooting around among the boxes. "Yes, well, you can't tell from the outside, can you? A lot of them haven't had anything shiny or good to eat, but lots have too!" He stuck his paw in a box and held up a sleek silver cell phone. "Look! I have a new phone. It's all mine."

I read the label on the torn edge of the box. "No, it's not. It belongs to this Bert Smashnik guy." I patted the dolly box. "And this is for—Mrs. Angela Atkins. I bet it's for her little girl. Her main Christmas present."

"And your point is?"

I was tempted to extend all of my points and let him see what they were, but didn't for two reasons. One is that he also has sharp claws and teeth, and is maybe a pound or two heavier than me. The other is that he is my friend and he can be useful. I just had to appeal to his better nature. If only I could find it.

"Renfrew, you don't even know how to use this stuff!" I told him, patting an iPad still in its package inside its box with the lid ripped off.

"I can feel it and wash it and make it shine!" he said. "And some of it looks like computers, and I can work computers better than you!" He flexed his hand-y paws at me.

"You can plug stuff in, but you can't really make them work," I told him. "Not out here in the woods. You need accounts and passwords and all kinds of stuff Darcy and Maddog and Bubba's partner have already."

"I could use the ones at your house," he said.

"Right. Of course you can. So why do you need to take somebody's Christmas present? I've spent my entire life learning how to use a computer, and there is quite a learning curve. Honestly, I don't think your—uh—temperament is suited for that kind of dull geeky stuff. I'll tell you what. If you'll help me return all these things before morning, I'll help you make a YouTube video showing how cute you are. You'll be a star."

He frowned, grumbled, and looked around at the litter with a very territorial gleam in his eye. "I don't think so, cat. This is mine. I stole it fair and square."

There was so much there, and I knew he'd lose interest before tomorrow, by which time it would all probably be ruined.

"Let me take the doll at least," I said. "She's not shiny, and you don't really want her, do you? Some poor little girl is going to be really sad tomorrow, and will probably grow up to hate Santa Claws thanks to this childhood trauma. She may even belong to a family that feeds raccoons now, but will become a hunter because she somehow suspects what became of her Christmas doll."

He stopped fiddling long enough to growl at me. "What do you care, cat? Why should you care if humans get what they want or not? You haven't seen what I've seen. There are cats and dogs wandering all over town, making nuisances of themselves, whose people abandoned them and moved away."

"Oh no! Why didn't you tell me? Is it vampires again? Are there more taking other people like the Vampire Marcel took Darcy?"

"I wish. No, they leave because they want to, and they abandon little Fluffikins or Fido because they want to."

"Renfrew, you've changed. You didn't used to hate humans."

"I don't hate them, but I've seen some stuff lately that—well, let's just say I don't care if they have a special happy day where they keep all their toys and I don't, even though they just left them on the porch."

He was justifying his selfishness by making it all someone else's fault, just like the bad guys on TV always did. I knew times were hard for humans. I'd heard Darcy on the phone to her friends talking about how tough it had been for people to get gifts, or even food for their families this year. It was on the news too. Some people may think it's un-catlike to care about that stuff, but I have always prided myself on being a *good* kitty. If nothing else, it makes me stand out from the crowd.

"You're just being a Scrooge," I told him.

He looked up. "What's that?"

"It's a mean old man in a story. He keeps seeing these ghosts, see . . ." I couldn't quite remember the whole thing, or which was the right version because since Halloween I'd seen the same story done about twenty different ways.

"What's a ghost?"

"Kind of like a vampire only deader, and without a body. They're very scary."

"Why if they don't have bodies? That's silly, being scared of those. Was the Scrooge scared of them?

"No, but they reminded him of stuff. Like some were—uh—the ghosts of the past. That was—er— animal friends who'd either died or been left behind come back to tell him to stop being such a jerk. Then there were the ghosts of Christmas present. I think those were people who found out coons were stealing the Christmas presents intended for their families. They all had ghostly guns. And then there's the ghosts of the future, and you don't even want to know what they did."

"Well, I don't know any ghosts. Just one noisy cat who's mad because he didn't like his present, and is trying to give it back. You can have something else if you want it. I've got lots. I'll even wash it for you to make it shinier."

"No thanks. I'm taking the doll, and then I'll be back and return the rest of the things where you got them," I told him. That was a lot easier said than done, however.

I picked up the package containing the doll box swimming in a shallow jumble of packing peanuts inside the wrapping. The address on the shredded outer cardboard was on Blair Street. That was mostly downhill, so I could drag the dolly, who was about as long and big around without the packaging as my tail. With the packaging, she was clumsy and caught on things, at least until I got out of the trees and onto the snowy path, where the box slid down to bump my nose and front feet as I tried to walk backwards.

I had just made the street when a striped blur waddled past me. "Change your mind?" I shouted after him, dropping the doll box. "How did you get this stuff to your nest anyway? It's heavy!" Some of the boxes in his stash were much bigger than the doll's.

He ignored me until he was way ahead of me on the sidewalk along Blair heading down toward the lagoon park. "Minions," he said. Then he turned, and I saw the shiny metal box he carried in one paw. "Needs washing," he added, with a white sharp grin under his black-mask.

It was just *so* wrong. My assistant detective apparently had hench-coons in his UPS bandit gang. This was really going to be bad for my corporate image as feline head of the premier interspecies detective agency of Port Deception. Mutiny! That's what it was. I wasn't about to let him get away with it! I dropped the doll box behind a convenient picket fence and took off down the sidewalk after the ring-tailed mutineer.

The snowy sidewalk was slick, so I jumped a fence and ran alongside it in the adjoining yards, jumping other fences when I needed to. I passed three dark houses and four with lights on them, fake trees lighted up, real trees lighted up, Santa and his sleigh with the—er—reindeer following the star heading for the hay. And in the next yard, there was the little farmyard scene I'd seen a few other places, with all the people in their bathrobes, clustered inside a three-sided carport. A fake star decorated the roof of the carport, and another bathrobed figure with wings hung above everybody else, plus some fake sheep, a fake donkey, and a horse trough-looking thing holding a doll. Maybe I should put Renfrew's doll in there?

The yard up ahead was dark. No car sat out front or in the driveway. A low fence separated the lit-up house from the dark one. I crossed into that yard and the next one, also dark, and sat to rest and reflect by having a wash beneath an overgrown hedge. Renfrew had no doubt already made it to the lagoon and ruined the shiny boxy thing's function, whatever it had been. I couldn't save all the presents. If I turned around now and went back to his nest and moved them all—took some of them home and stuck them in the house—that would save some of them anyway, and he wouldn't be there to stop me.

That seemed like a good plan. If the owl had been sitting in a tree when it saw me, which is, I understand, the way owls usually spot someone tasty to eat, I wouldn't have heard it and would have been a dead cat on a one-way flight to an owl's nest. But he was on the ground, watching, and when he spotted me and came after me instead of the less accessible prey he'd been hoping would come out

and play, the other prey found her voice and let out a long, low growl. The noise tipped me off, my excellent feline instincts for avoiding air strikes kicked in, and I dived for cover deeper into the hedge.

The owl flapped and hooted a little, and I made myself *very* big, slitted my eyes, arched my back and sprang right at his wide-open eyes.

Oh, yeah, he had talons and a razor sharp beak, but he generally used them on animals dangling helplessly from his talons, not head-on. "Back off, bozo!" I spat at him.

The owl blinked at me, taken aback, his head retreating while his body stayed in the same place. I guess he wasn't used to his snacks talking back. "I beg your pardon," he said. "I mistook you for someone else. No need to get huffy. I have to eat too, you know." And with a ground-dragging unfurling of his massive wings, each of them at least as long as I am from nose to tail tip, he was airborne.

I didn't trust him to stay gone, not for a moment. But I wasn't about to stay inside the hedge all night, and I wanted to find the other cat who had warned me of the attack.

"Hello there," I called. "Where are you? The owl's gone, at least for now. I scared him away."

"Meaa?" The sound was weak and faint. Another voice, maybe responding to the alarm in the mother's voice, added, "Me me me . . ." Okay, a queen with a kitten. But where?

I crawled out far enough to look around. "Do that again," I prompted.

This time there was another growl. And without the owl in the way, I smelled the blood, and my lips curled up. The sound and the smell both came from a rickety wooden step joining the bottom of the house to the ground. I looked around, didn't see the owl, and in a flash faster than Renfrew could empty a kibble dish, made a four-point landing in front of the step. Hunkering down in the gathering snow, I slunk on my belly to the shallow opening. I stuck my nose in and jerked it back out again, narrowly avoiding the slashing claws of the cat inside.

"Whoa!" I said. "I'm on your side. What's going on? Did the owl try to take your mouse?"

"Mouse?" she asked.

"Meep!" a small voice squeaked. It wasn't claiming to be a mouse. It smelled new and catty and bloody, and its cry was puny and shrill. "This is my kitten," the queen said proudly. "There was another one, but it died. I just had this one, and I will tear you to shreds if you try to hurt her you—you tomcat, you."

"Why would I do something like that?" I asked. "Some of my best friends used to be kittens, back when I was one. Please, may I come under there too? I don't know how long that owl will stay gone." She didn't say anything, so I scooted a claw length forward with each paw and asked, "Why are you and your kitten out here? It's snowing."

"Is that so?" she asked. "Do you think we wouldn't be inside if we could be? This used to be my house. I'm no stray. A family with a little girl came to my mother when I was a baby and brought me here to live with them and be a friend for the little girl. She dressed me up in doll clothes. I really hated that, but I wouldn't mind one of those doll blankets now, I can tell you. My poor baby is so c-cold."

I heard rat-like scrabblings next to her and an occasional *meep* as the blind kitten stumbled. Its cries were quavery. "If you'll let me come in, I'll lie beside you and warm your baby. You can tell me all about it. And I'm not *exactly* a tomcat. Darcy took me to the vet as soon as I was old enough so I can't make kittens."

"Are you sure?" she asked. "The last cat who told me that fathered this one!" Her eyes widened as I blocked some of the light, pulling myself inside, and lay down with my head facing the opposite direction from hers so my tail wrapped around her front and her kitten. The hole went all the way through beneath the step so I could see out the other side.

"You look a little like him, as a matter of fact," she said, shifting her kitten to a position more comfortable for her. She was a gray-brown tabby whose fur was still matted with rapidly freezing blood and other fluids from giving birth. I snuggled in so that the nursing kitten was sandwiched between us, causing it to "meep" again. "His fur wasn't as nice though. You do have a lovely coat."

"Thanks," I said. "I think I know the cat you're talking about. He's my father too. Your kitten is my half-sister." It may be hard for humans to tell the sex of kittens, but I could smell it. "He makes a lot of kittens, and most of us look like him. I've met him though. Kind of nasty."

"Not if you're a female in heat," she said. "Not at first. He got a little rough later, but I sent him off with a nose full of claws. Then my people decided to move. I think Maddy, my little girl, had convinced them to take me with them when they moved; but then when I got pregnant, they just went off and left me. Maybe if they come back and see I only had the one kitten, they'll take me with them." Her voice broke, and she disguised her distress by licking her kitten. "They've been gone a really long time, and don't seem to have told anyone else to look after me."

I was so busy listening to her, feeling sorry for her, wondering if I should tell her what Rocky told me: that her people were probably gone for good and wouldn't be back, that I didn't hear the wings until *what to my wondering eyes did appear?* Long claws of an owl, entirely too near!

17

The new mom shivered, but I puffed up as big as I could within the confines of the hole and growled. "I thought I told you to hit the clouds, bird! Pfssst!"

The owl didn't answer this time, but his claws vanished for a split second—then I heard them overhead, on the step, ripping at the rotting wood. One splintering moment later his large eye peered down at us through the hole in the stair. "More than one way to skin a cat," he said.

"I can't believe you said that in front of the children!" I scolded.

"I only see the one tender little kitten," he said. I was glad owls couldn't lick their beaks and drool, or he'd have been doing that, and it was disgusting.

"She's not even a beak-full to you," I said, letting my mouth do the sparring while I figured out what to do with the rest of me—and him. "She's just newborn and hasn't even opened her eyes yet, so she can't be properly terrified of you. Her mom has had a hard time." It had worked with an eagle I met earlier to tell her about how bad I'd be for her and her babies since while I'm organic I am not exactly additive free, but the owl wasn't raising babies, and he didn't give a hoot.

He inserted his talons into the hole and ripped a strip from the stair. I was at a loss for the first time in my young life, really. I am a very clever cat, but he was a very large bird, and I was more impressed than ever with his claws, seeing them at such close range. I could slip outside and attack him, but I hardly had the advantage of surprise. Plus there was nothing to stop him, once I moved, from snatching both the kitten and her mother out of the hole and flying off with them before I could wriggle all the way out from under the stair.

"I want you to think about this carefully," I told the owl. "You have the reputation for being a wise old bird." Inspiration struck. "You *do* realize this is Christmas, don't you?"

"Why, yes. And as soon as I smelled your friends there, I thought to myself, "Merry Christmas to who? Me!""

"Well, you're not doing it right," I told him.

"What?"

"Christmas. Wise creatures aren't supposed to eat babies for Christmas."

"Is that so? I would settle for adult housecat if you keep getting in my way."

"You, you, you. You're messing up the story. Think about your place in history."

"How's that?" At least he didn't ask "who?" He looked genuinely curious. As I suspected, owls didn't get wise by declining to acquire new data.

"Wise—uh—things, are supposed to bring presents to babies at Christmas. Check those scenes in some of the yards around here if you don't believe me. You go on and check it out. We're not moving."

He wasn't that full of scientific curiosity though.

"Yes, I'm afraid you are. Keep talking though. The hot air you're spouting will give my wings extra lift when it's time to carry you to my nest."

He ripped another strip off and looked at my beautiful gold striped body with what struck me as an unwholesome appetite. "You're a plump one. If I take you, I can come back for the other two later. Nothing personal, you understand. We're all hunters here, yes?" He jerked back suddenly, flapping and whirling in a feathered storm. "Who? Who's there?"

"Hey there, big bird, but have you seen a cat around here? Maybe carrying a doll or dragging a box?"

The owl flapped and sat back on the step he'd been destroying so that some of his tail feathers tickled my nose, and I sneezed.

"This is my lucky day," the owl said. "Cats of all sizes, and now a big fat raccoon."

"Hey!" Renfrew said. "Be nice! I am worth way more than a meal. I have treasures. Shiny treasures. Like this!" The owl moved away, and I could see out a hole that had opened in the side of the step when the top of the step was ripped open. The snow had stopped, and bright moonlight now reflected alluringly from the surface of the freshly washed metal box thingy in the coon's paw.

The owl was on him—or on where he had been—in one hop. Renfrew, however, was out on the sidewalk and halfway up the street squealing his head off.

I hollered too, and the mom cat hissed, "If you're going to carry on like that, get away from us."

"I'm calling for help," I told her.

"I've cried and cried for help, and all that I get is things that want to eat me," she mewed.

That didn't discourage me, but I didn't argue with her. *I'd* come to help her after all, hadn't I? "Can you carry your kitten?"

"Of course I can! I'm her mother!"

"We need to find a better hiding place for you," I said with a meaningful look at the stars shining down through the hole the owl had ripped in the step. "Maybe under the house?"

"I can't go there," she said. "I thought of that when my people first left. There are big rats in there—bigger than I am. They would kill my kitten."

"Mrrr," I said, thinking. "Pick her up and walk with me. Well, trot if you can. We need to cross a couple of yards."

Renfrew had either been eaten by the owl, or had eaten the owl, or both of them were really busy picking through his new treasure. They weren't in sight as we crossed the darkened yards. The queen tottered with the kitten and had to stop twice to rest, but refused my offer to carry her baby for her.

Finally we made it to the carport, which was where I thought maybe they would be safer, under the roof, amid all of the stone people, who might scare the owl, and up off the ground in the horse trough thing.

I was surprised now to see Buck's antlers alongside the lit-up deer in the yard, and Nelda and Gelda grazing beside him.

It made me feel better that friends were there. Not that they could be depended upon to defend the new mother. They're pretty shy. Still, I said, "Hi, deer—uh—Merry Christmas. Good to see you here. This is, uh—"

"La Toya," the mother cat said through a mouthful of kitten.

"La Toya and her new kitten. An owl has been after her, and so I thought if she got up in that thing—"

"That's a manger, Spam," Nelda said. "It's where the hay was in the original story. The hay the reindeer seek every Christmas as they fly through the sky following the star."

"Yes, the manger." La Toya needed a little boost to help her jump up into the hay—there was real hay—but she managed it and laid down, exhausted.

I wanted to do the same thing, but felt like I needed to stand guard at least until morning.

"You planning on grazing here long?" I asked Nelda.

"It's nice grass," she said. "Still green and moist under the snow."

"Could you wake me up before you go or if an owl comes, or a coyote?" I asked. "I really need a nap."

"Of course, Spam. When you wake up, it will be Christmas morning, and we may be flying off into the sky with the reindeer. But I'll be sure and let you know first."

I can sleep anywhere if I want to, and I decided to rest on top of the fake camel. I forgot to say there was a fake camel, but there was, and I slept between his neck and his hump.

A pungent, and yet oddly familiar scent awoke me, I'm not sure how much later. But Nelda and her family were not there, as they'd promised, and my old man with his matted, tattered coat was peeing on the perimeter of the makeshift manger and chatting up La Toya.

"So, sweetheart, just one kitten, eh? I'm slipping. Used to get five or six at a whack every time."

"You told me you were fixed! And now my people have abandoned me and our daughter!"

Dad laughed. "It's not all that bad. Come with me. Join the clowder. My other mates will show you the ropes, help you take care of the kitten, and you'll be just fine without people. Take a break now, and I'll tell you all about it. See, there are lots of ways to get fed when you're wild and free without having to put up with people. I can show you one if you come have breakfast with me."

He turned tail and headed for the back yard. Looking over his shoulder at her he called, "Come on, honeybunch. Lately they've been serving a regular buffet here for all us homeless kitty cats. Sonny boy, you stay here with the kid. It's about all you're good for since the humans got a hold of you."

"Maybe I'd like to eat too," I said. I didn't feel I was cut out to be a mother, or even a kitten sitter.

La Toya looked at me pleadingly. She'd told me she hadn't eaten in days, and she'd need to in order to feed the kid. I knew where my kibble bowl was at home, and if I acted really pitiful, could probably get Darcy to break out the good stuff.

I shrugged my whiskers. With a little growl at the smug and very male hind quarters of my old man, slinging his excess baggage under his tail, I jumped up in the manger, and she jumped down. "I'll watch the kid," I told her. "Hurry back."

I curled up next to the doll in the manger with the kitten between us. It squalled a couple of times, and then tried to nurse in my long fur. Most of the kitten was buried in my coat, which kept it warm at least. It kneaded and kneaded, its tiny little paws massaging my side. Soothing. Maybe being a mother wasn't such a bad job. I grew a little drowsy. La Toya and the old man were sure taking their time about eating. I hoped what was keeping them wasn't what I feared might be keeping them. Poor La Toya hadn't been fixed yet, and she still had one kitten to raise— could she even START a new litter before this baby was out of the nest? I licked the kitten on the part not buried in my belly fur. "I'll try to talk her out of it, kid," I told the baby. "She wouldn't like the rough life he leads, and would spend a lot of it trying to protect you from those other females he thinks would take care of you. He knows how to make kittens, and that's it. My human would probably take you two in if I got your Mom to bring you to the door. Maybe it would be best if I carried you, and she just came with us. I mean, you can't do without your mother, but if I was carrying you in my mouth, and pawed the door and looked up at my human with big sad eyes, what's she going to do? Resist me *and* a baby kitten and a pretty young queen? I don't furry think so. Not *my* Darcy." Okay, it was kind of a one-sided conversation. But it's never too early to instill family values in the young.

I was actually talking to the kitten to try to keep myself awake. It seemed like hours since the old man and La Toya took off for the back yard. The night was clearer and colder, I was exhausted, and the kitten

was actually quite a soothing little thing. It was very .
. .

"Coyote!" Gelda cried, and the deer scattered. At almost the same instant, from the back yard, there was a loud "Clang!" and the spitting, hissing, yowling of angry cats. I hoped the coyote would eat the old man first, I thought, believing it was the cause of the commotion behind the house.

So I was looking the wrong way and didn't really see the coyote until it was eye-to-eye with me.

I must have jumped back, the kitten still attached at the mouth to my fur.

The coyote licked its chops. "An entree and dessert all on the same plate!" the coyote said, slavering.There had always been someone between me and coyotes before. Bubba the police dog, Rocky .
.

Somehow I hissed, snarled, and caterwauled for, "Rocky!" at the same time.

The coyote leaped for me, snapping its jaws where my head used to be. I sat back on my tail, ready to snatch up the kitten and head for the shoulders of the nearest statue.

The coyote lunged again, giving me a whiff of his rancid garbage breath. The wind from his snapping jaws blew back my fur, which was sticking straight out from all my follicles.

The kitten suddenly lost her grip on me and tumbled out the back of the manger onto the porch step.

New plan! I flew in the face of the coyote, going right for his nose and eyes with all claws deployed and raking.

The coyote snarled in return, and I gave him another smack on the nose. Then suddenly he flew into the air, bawling, "Kiyi! Kiyi! Kiyi!"

He snapped, growled and squirmed, but it had nothing to do with me.

Behind his head I saw the transformed batlike ears of my roomie, the vampcat—or catpire, take your pick—Rocky, who had been a creature of the night ever since he bit the vampire who was invading our house. With his supernatural strength, the battered old tom held the coyote by the throat in midair while he drained his blood with really rather disgusting slurpy sounds.

I jumped from the manger to the step to comfort the kitten, who was okay, except for staggering around saying, "me, meep, me, meep!" looking for me or her mom.

Rocky bore the coyote to ground, sucking away until the doggy creature was quivering and cowering and crying. I was no longer worried about Mr. Coyote. Since Rocky had become a catpire, the predators who had once scared the poop out of him when he was on his own in the wild were now his very favorite prey. He loved seeking them out to harass and feed on at every opportunity.

He gave the one at his feet a clout on the nose, and said, "Get outta here. I'm not gonna kill you on accounta there's children present. But find yourself some new territory, hound dog, because if I ever catch you near another cat, I'll finish what I started." As an afterthought, he added, "Mewaahahahaha-hahah."

The coyote cringed.

I spat at him and washed my shoulder as if flicking off the spot of bother he had caused me before meeting my friends in high places. He skulked off as fast as he could go with his tail tucked between his legs.

With a lash of his tail, Rocky went airborne again, and for a moment hovered in front of the bathrobed human with the wings at the top of the carport. "Any more trouble, just sing out, kit," he said to me.

28

"Thanks, pal," I replied. "You're a life-saver."

He melted back into the night.

The deer gingerly tip-hoofed their way back toward the yard. I picked up the kitten as gently as I could by the scruff of the neck and turned toward the back yard to see what was left of La Toya and the old man. I didn't know what the yowling and clanging had been about, but I was sure if La Toya were still alive she'd have come when I started snarling in her kitten's defense.

Good thing the kitten didn't have her eyes open yet so she wouldn't have to see her mama all messed up and bloody. Except—wait. There was no smell of blood, only angry but healthy cats. All was, in fact, quiet now in the back yard. A big rectangular box sat on the lawn under the bird feeder. Cat snores rattled the wire front. Carrying the kitten closer, I saw the latch at the bottom. It would have made a clang when it slammed shut.

My old man and La Toya lay together in a furry puddle near the back of the cage. The scent of salmon still perfumed the air, but not a scale remained inside the cage.

I set the kitten down on the grass, and she clung to my leg, trying to nurse on my toes. A skim of snow covered the ground with the grass spiking up through it. I rowled at La Toya, but she didn't wake up. See if I ever kitten-sat for her again! I rowled again. She thrust one paw out, then the other, stretched forward, then put her rump up and stretched back. Her eyes opened, and I think it was then that she remembered she was a new mother. Or maybe it was when her back end went in the air and she realized it was still sore from giving birth.

"How did my kitten get out there?" she asked.

"The question is how you got in there," I told her. But I thought I knew. I had heard Darcy's new boy-riend the shelter dude/Sheriff's deputy (who was *not* a vampire) talking about the live traps Olympic Mountain Rescue set out for feral cats, baiting them with food and letting the cats enjoy the chow for several days before setting the trap to spring. The wily old con cat who sired me and half the kittens in town had finally been conned himself. Good. And it might be a good thing for La Toya to be taken to the shelter and let her rest up and get some food—except that if she weren't there for this newborn kitten, the baby was for sure gonna die, because Uncle Spammy did not have the required equipment to help her out.

Small as the kitten was, it was too big to stick through the wire mesh of the cage door. I hoped the people would come soon and pick up the trap. They wouldn't take me, or if they did, they wouldn't keep me because I had a personal ID chip that also let me in my personal entrance to my personal home. But I wasn't sure the kitten could survive in the cold this long.

The kitten was shivering badly now from being out in the air. The sky was lightening, and I could see a thin fuzz of ginger among the white fuzz on her. She was going to be another orange tabby, like me, and like the old man would have been if he weren't such a matted mess.

La Toya didn't help matters. She started crying and crying and crying. She woke up the old man, who started cussing in cat, which sounds a lot like crying, only louder. "Maybe you two could shut up?" I said. "You're safe from predators, but the kid and I aren't . . ."

La Toya shut up, and with a final growl, so did my pop, though he continued to pace and mutter furiously.

"The snow isn't good for the baby," I told them. "I'm taking her back to the manger. Then I'm going to shred that door, and wake up those people to come out and get the trap and the kitten."

I snuggled next to the kitten letting her warm up in my fur again and pretend to nurse. She shivered for a long time. After all she and her mother had been through, and now with them separated, I began to worry. What if she didn't make it?

According to the Critter Channel there were too many kittens already, and a lot of them didn't survive infancy. But those kittens weren't ones I was taking care of. I purred as loudly as I could to reassure the little thing and worried myself into a doze. Then I really had to pee, so I jumped down and poised to go on the floor of the carport.

The owl sailed into the enclosure and perched on the side of the manger, cocking his head first to one side, and then the other, studying the kitten, who was kind of bumbling around like *It* in a game of hide and seek. I was frozen. This was it. After all we'd been through, I wasn't close enough to reach the kitten before the owl could eat her. I started to growl, but then instead of slashing at the kitten with his beak, the owl, put his beak to his own wing and plucked out a feather, allowing it to drift down onto the kitten's ear. The little one raised a feeble paw, tried to bat the feather, and fell over.

The owl said, in a formal kind of way. "I'm sorry I tried to eat you. The coon explained to me that it's unwise to eat someone born on such an auspicious day, and furthermore, bad luck. That the custom is to give them gifts instead. So here's one of my personal feathers. Should you ever need me at any time, just lick the feather, and I'll help you however I can—and won't eat you before, during or after." He bent down and winked at me. "You explain it to the kid when she's old enough, okay? You cats have a nice day."

I was about to hop back into the manger when the door opened behind me, and a woman wearing a puffy purple jacket over pajamas and gardening

boots bustled out and headed to the cage in the back yard, without seeing me or the kitten. I returned to the kitten and waited, and pretty soon, here she came, hauling the cage. She'd put a blanket over it. I sat up and meowed for her attention, pawing at the air just in case she was deaf.

"Hello, handsome. What's the matter? You didn't climb aboard before the door shut?"

She set down the cage to pet me—and maybe add me to her catch, I don't know, and I moved aside so she could see the kitten. La Toya mewed piteously, which could almost be heard.

"Oh," the woman said. "Oh, dear. Well, this is different. We'll have to go inside and sort this out." She picked up the kitten and stuck her in one of the jacket pockets and picked up the cage again. I decided I had done about all I could do and that I didn't have time to get taken into custody and released again. It was Christmas, and according to the older cats, there were treats and new toys to be had at home.

Home seemed a very long way away however. The woman didn't grab for me, but held open the door so I could go inside too. I guess she had decided I wasn't feral because of the very brave and confident way I acted with her. I declined her gracious invitation, and before she had the carrier inside, had hit the sidewalk and was two houses away.

I was very tired. I had not had my customary five or six rejuvenating naps that night while staying alert against possible threats to La Toya and her kitten. Had it not been so cold, I'd have found a nice little spot to curl up and sleep. But it was cold, and Christmas morning was here. I pattered up the sidewalk, but confess my tail had less than its usual perky curl, and the light hurt my eyes. It's not surprising that I missed noticing what was not there, under the circumstances.

Nelda's little herd stood grazing at the edge of the woods.

"Oh, Spam," she said, her tone in my mind a bit whispery. "The coyote didn't get you. Good."

"Thanks for the backup," I said, a little sarcastically. The coyote might be a supreme predator, but the deer were bigger and had very sharp hooves—and Buck had antlers. They might have helped a little.

"You're very welcome. Good thing we were there to warn you."

I felt sorry for being so grouchy and rubbed against her slender front legs. "Thanks." They were deer, after all, and almost always bolted at the least threat. "Rocky took care of the coyote."

"Oh, good."

Gelda said, "You are a tired kitty, aren't you? A long night?"

"You know it. I've been on the move, busy all the time, since I saw you guys last night."

"Want a ride?" she offered. The deer had let me ride them before in an emergency, but had made it clear they were not a cat taxi service. "In honor of the reindeer and the manger."

I jumped onto her back, my front paws around her neck, my back ones straddling her back. And I was out of it until, almost at the upper edge of the woods, I heard Darcy calling me. "Spam! Spammy! Come and get it, kitty! There's goodies!"

I said, "Merry—uh—hay manger, Gelda!" and started to jump down, but she said, "Wait, cat. The street is dangerous. I am bigger. Let me cross." And she carried me over saying, "Merry Manger to you too, cat."

Darcy stood at our door, clutching her sweater tight around her. I started to jump into her arms, but noticed one of her hands was occupied—a tattered brown box with bubble wrap poking out. She caught my look and bent down and picked me up, juggling her package. "Just because you can go out whenever you want to doesn't mean you should stay out, Spammy. I was worried." She kissed my head between my ears and buried her face in my fur. She smelled nice, and I knew she was fresh out of the shower. I started the arduous task of marking her with my scent all over again, starting with cheek rubs.

She carried me inside, dropping the package on the table, and me on the floor. I made straight for the food dish. The kibble was low. I looked up at Darcy, who was messing with her package and wearing a puzzled expression.

Deputy Shelter Dude walked into the kitchen from the living room. "Anything the matter?"

"No, Spam's back, but—there was a package on the stoop, kind of beat up. My cousin in Minneapolis sent it a month ago and gave me the tracking number. It should have been here two weeks ago."

"That is one messed up package," he said. "Maybe it got lost in the mail, or shredded in one of the machines . . ."

"But nobody delivers on Christmas Day," she said. "Hmmm."

"Maybe it went to a neighbor by mistake and they dropped it off."

"Yeah, probably."

Somewhere, a dog barked. It turned out to be in DSD's jacket. "Sorry, I gotta go," he said. "Don't suppose you want to come with me?"

"What's going on, Daryl?"

"Three new cats coming in—a very small half-frozen female and her newborn. Amanda Baker says it's a wonder the kitten made it since somehow she trapped the mother, but not the baby. It would have frozen, but another big fluffy cat was curled up with it in the manger in the nativity scene in their carport."

"I wish she had a picture of that!" Darcy said, casting a quick look at me. She knows from personal experience that I have skills not possessed by my siblings. "You said three cats?"

"Yeah, a big male, definitely feral. Badly matted coat. Ginny's going to come in tomorrow morning and do his surgery and shots."

His surgery? The old man was not going to like that.

As they left, I skinned out the door with them and hopped into Deputy Daryl's car and onto Darcy's lap. Deputy Daryl had been present during my final showdown with the vampire when I had to save Darcy, so he didn't question my motives any more than Darcy did. I got some extra petting on the way. The car warmed up before we reached the end of the block.

The lady from the house with the manger was waiting for us, the big cage set beside her, and a smaller carrier on the other side. Both cage and carrier had colorful fleece blankets thrown over them so the cats could have some privacy. Daryl let us in the shelter. The minute we were inside La Toya began crying, and the old man's cage rocked furiously as he scratched, tore and pounded at the heavy wire. While the people were talking, I stuck my nose under the blanket of La Toya's carrier. She and the kitten were inside, the kitten nursing, but she was panting heavily, stressed. "Oh, Spam, what's going to happen to us? Will they take my kitten? Will we be killed? Who are these humans and why did they take us?" Her cries were growing shriller and shriller.

"La Toya, shush. All this yelling isn't good for the baby. You're going to scare her too. Don't worry. My human lady knows the man here, and I've found out a little more about this place. They only want us cats to be looked after, make sure we get food and water and don't get sick or anything. Lots of times cats who come here find new humans to live with. You'd like that, wouldn't you?"

"Who needs them?" she said. "Hank said I'm better off living wild and free with his clowder."

"Yeah, well, Hank told you a lot of things before, didn't he?" I asked, guessing that Hank must be the name my old man used.

"I'm so afraid," she said with a small piteous mew and a shiver.

Darcy knelt down, removing the blanket and petting me as she checked out La Toya and her baby. "Spammy, that kitten is going to look like you and your brothers when it's a little older," she said. I wished I could tell her who else the kitten would look like too. "Would it be okay with you if we take these two home with us so I can make sure the kitten gets what she needs? They're a little fragile to stay here with the rest of the cats all night, especially by themselves. I'd have to put them in the office."

I purred. Normally the office was off limits to the other cats, being my territory, but the truth was, now that I had my own entrance, I wasn't in there as much as I used to be.

I turned back to La Toya, "Darcy—that's my lady—wants to take you home. You'll be okay. There are lots of other cats there."

"What if they hate me? What if they try to kill my baby? I've heard that happens sometimes!"

"I'll be there, and my mother too. We'll see to it that you're treated right. They're a good bunch."

"LET MEYOWWWWT!!!" The old man—Hank— hollered at the top of his lungs, rocking the cage back and forth.

I poked my nose under his blanket, and almost got it sliced as he tried to bend the wire like

39

Superman. "Cut it out," I said. "You're scaring the baby."

He growled and snarled like a wildcat, but I was stern—it was easy to be with him inside the cage and me out. "I mean it, Hank. If you'll shut up for a minute somebody will put you in a bigger cage and . . ."

"I don't belong in a cage!" he roared. "I have to be free! The minute they open this I am out of here."

He wasn't, of course. It might have been harder if the other cats hadn't chimed in. "Will you look there, Myrtle? It's Prince Charming himself!" One of the lady cats sneered.

"Oh yeah. Hey, handsome, do you ever see any of my kittens anymore? You sure haven't been back to see how we were!"

"Yeah, I got kicked out of my house because you knocked me up," another one complained.

"They dumped me in a parking lot to die," said another one. "It's all your fault."

"Not my fault," he cried back, this time on the defensive. "It's those humans! You should never have trusted them."

"Humans don't give you kittens, Slick. Tomcats give you kittens. Well, I hear they fix that in here."

"*What?*" he jumped—and landed in the new cage, where Daryl, Darcy and Amanda meant for him to go. The capture cage was decorated like a Christmas tree with clumps of his matted fur and streaks of blood.

"You're getting snipped, Stud," Myrtle, a calico with one red eye, told him, lashing her tail.

"Snipped?" he asked.

"Don't let them scare you, Hank," I told him, suddenly a little sorry for the old man in the midst of all of these vengeful queens. "It doesn't amount to much. All the males at my house have had it done, and it doesn't really make any difference. You just can't make kittens anymore."

"How do you know my name?" he demanded suspiciously. "Wait—wait, I know you. You said you were my kid. I met you down at Sea-J's, trying to move in on the clowder's fish franchise. Is this your twisted idea of revenge?"

"No," I said.

"Spam, we're going now. Are you coming?"

I looked back at Darcy, who had the carrier with La Toya and the kitten in her hand. La Toya wasn't crying now. In fact, I think she was laughing— probably at Hank's predicament. But terror rolled off him like an incoming tide, and the females were not making it easier, of course. They were imagining what his surgery would be like in gory detail while he wailed and railed against them.

When I trotted back to Darcy and rubbed her legs he squatted in a corner bawling.

"I gotta get out of here," Daryl said. "Poor old guy."

I jumped up on the second tier of cages, where the old man cowered, and sat on top of his cell, which wasn't very comfortable, since it wasn't a solid surface. Darcy took off her sweater and shoved it on top of the cage for me to lie on. "Spam wants to stay with him." She caressed my head and ears with her hand. "We'll be back for you in the morning, sweetie."

"Who asked you to stick around?" Hank asked as they left.

"Nobody," I said. "But I'm going to anyway."

"So you can see what they do to me? Like those females?"

"They won't do it right away," I said. "They'll give you your shots and probably trim your mats—they might wait till they put you out to do that though."

"Put me out? You mean like put me to sleep? Like the long sleep?"

"No. Not kill you. Just help you go to sleep so you don't feel any pain when they do the snip. It makes your legs not work right for a while and you walk funny, but it'll be okay. They're just trying to make you healthy. And really, you don't need to make any more kittens. You could have stopped with me, as far as I'm concerned."

"This is so unfair. I am a leader among cats, father of my race, a mighty warrior . . ."

"You're more a deadbeat dad than anything," I said, then remembered another part of the seasonal stories I'd been seeing on TV and the internet. "Think of me as the spirit of kittens past. La Toya's baby is kittens present. And if you keep on doing what you do, before long there will be so many orange kittens and cats, there won't be any more prey, and wild cats like you will be eating each other to survive. They usually eat the old feeble cats first, I hear." I was just making that up, but somehow I needed to convince him that changing his ways, however involuntarily, was a good thing—or at least the lesser evil.

"You are awfully damn sure of yourself for a kid," he said.

"My mother saw to it that we have a safe home with Darcy—my lady who took La Toya. I've had a good education. Not all of your kits are going to get that chance."

"Thank Bast. One of you is enough."

"Is that so? Then why didn't you stop at one?"

"Son, my seed spreading is not a character flaw. A tom's gotta do what a tom's gotta do."

"All the more reason to retire, Pop."

"My clowder won't respect me anymore."

"Maybe not, but when they get trapped, you can let them know it's not the end of the line for them. Like I'm trying to do with you."

"Why? I thought you hated me." He had stopped snarling now, and his ears had gone from laid back to kind of flat out to the sides of his head, sad-looking really. His voice was a little whiny, but I figured that was understandable, under the circumstances.

"No, Pop. I don't even know you, really. But maybe when you get back to the clowder again, we can help each other out sometimes."

"Help how?"

I think I actually put him to sleep telling him about me and Darcy and the vampire, Renfrew, Maddog, the deer and everything. I at least shut up the lady cats, who stopped bawling at him to listen to my story. Eventually I put me to sleep too. But we awoke once, and my old man had put his nose up to mine. He was purring, finally. "You okay, Dad?" I asked him.

He ignored my question, saying, "You ever caught a fish with your paw, Junior? When this is over, come down to the dock, and I'll show you."

"It's a deal," I said.

I stayed with him till he met Dr. Ginny later that afternoon. Always the ladies' man, he took a shine to her. "You go home and make sure your little sister's okay, Spam," the old man said.

When Ginny put him in her car to go to the clinic for his snip, she gave me a lift home. I was just in time to play with the boxes and the crinkled balls of wrapping paper with my brothers, until I finally fell asleep again in one of the boxes.

THE END

About the Authors

K.B. Dundee, known to his friends as Kittibits, ruled the Scarborough household for 16 years as head cat and union steward. Now residing at the Rainbow Bridge, Dundee remains a feline activist dedicated to cats' rights and making sure humans do as they are supposed to. This is not his first collaboration with his human, but is the first one where she gives him proper credit. He says that Spam is handling this situation exactly as he would have done, but Scarborough says no, Kittibits would have hidden under the bed.

Elizabeth Ann Scarborough is the author of 23 solo fantasy and science fiction novels, including the 1989 Nebula award winning HEALER'S WAR, loosely based on her service as an Army Nurse in Vietnam during the Vietnam War. She has collaborated thus far on 16 novels with Anne McCaffrey, six in the best selling Petaybee series and eight in the YA bestselling Acorna series, and most recently, the Tales of the Barque Cat series, *Catalyst* and *Catacombs* (from Del Rey). Recently she has converted all of her previously published solo novels to eBooks with the assistance of Gypsy Shadow Publishing, under her own Fortune imprint. SPAM VS THE VAMPIRE is her first exclusive novel for eBook and print on demand publication.

Website: http://www. eascarborough.com

About the Cover Artist/Illustrator

Karen Gillmore's art career began in Seattle, Washington, in 1974. Her many adventures have included ten years selling her drawings and jewelry at Seattle's Pike Place Market, traveling the US from coast to coast on the street fair circuit, theatre and costume design, and a variety of illustration commissions. Karen immigrated to Canada in 1992, where she took up printmaking and began exploring mixed media, collage, and photography. Recently she has returned to illustration, and has illustrated two books about tidepools and a growing number of e-book covers, and has her sights set on creating graphic novels. Karen also exhibits her work in gallery settings and teaches art classes.

Artist statement:

"My favorite mediums for illustration are watercolour, graphite and coloured pencils, and pen and ink, often in combination with each other. I also use acrylic and linocut, and occasionally go on collage binges, in which my studio ends up wall-to-wall and ceiling-to-floor paper-and-glue bits. I like to work 3-dimensionally for fun, usually in papier maché. My subject matter ranges from Celtic knotwork and magical creatures to landscape and figure studies. Aided and advised by my trusty cat Mak, who also sometimes models for me, I especially like drawing and sculpting cats and other fuzzy people.

"I am inordinately fond of felines, sea creatures large and small, and trees, and I love to garden and sing and play an eclectic selection of folk music on a bunch of instruments. I write music and poetry in my copious spare time. Beaches and mountains are my favorite places, and I bend time and space to be able to spend time there."

Afterword

All proceeds from the sale of the electronic version of this book will go to benefit the Humane Society of Jefferson County, WA's Safehaven Shelter. The profits (after expenses) from the print book will also go to benefit the shelter.

For the last five years this shelter has operated with a no-kill policy for all healthy animals. They also have five office cats, one of whom was born with a neurological condition that causes him to bump into things and sometimes walk in circles.

Mr. Dundee and Ms. Scarborough began their partnership at the shelter at its old location in a cinderblock building along a country road near Scarborough's residence. Her beloved Mr. Peaches, who had come down with her from Alaska, was 20 years old when he died from diabetes and kidney failure. Scarborough says, "I was depressed and hardly felt like getting up in the morning with no Peachy to greet me. I wanted to get another orange kitten as much like him as possible, but I had to make another extended trip and didn't want to introduce a kitten when I'd have to be gone. Although I had other cats, Peaches was my best buddy and I missed him terribly. Then the woman who had been taking care of him and my other cats while I was in Ireland decided she wanted a cat of her own and adopted one from the shelter. Her car broke down and she asked me to drive her to the shelter to pick up paperwork for her cat so he could get his neutering discount at the vet's.

"I was a good cat addict and stayed in the car while she went in, like an alcoholic avoiding the temptation of a bar. But pretty soon she came out cuddling a kitten in her coat so I could admire him.

That did it. I had to go in and see the other kittens. I was doing pretty well scanning the cat cages and being very hard, saying, "Nope, too manic, too shy, too young, too old," with my hand down by my side. Then I felt a little soft paw reach out and snag my finger and a kitten tongue start to give it a good wash. I bent down to see who my groomer was and saw a beautiful little kitten, marked just like Peaches but with Maine Coon characteristics similar to those I'd seen on my friend Anne McCaffrey's pure bred Maine Coons in Ireland.

"Peaches died in my arms and when he did, I told him that if he wanted to come back as a cat, somehow let me know and I would bring him home again. So I told the Peaches-esque little furball, 'Okay, message received. Come on back home.' I named him Bonnie Dundee for the town in Scotland where I'd attended a wonderful folk festival. They also make some of the world's best orange marmalade there, and as you can see, Dundee is what they call an orange marmalade cat in British novels. Bonnie Dundee, Lord Claverhouse, is a Scottish historical personage from that area. My suspicions about Peaches recycling himself as a similar kitten were confirmed by Dundee, who went straight to all of Peachy's favorite nap places, toys, and food dishes, much like the new Dalai Lama does with each incarnation to convince the rinpoches that he is the right candidate for the job. But because he was so tiny, his heroic name seemed a little large for him, so he became Kittibits. I did take my trip, with him at home waiting quite impatiently for me to return. I could hear him yowling his head off every time I called home to check on my cat family.

"Now, one of the interesting things to me about Kittibits and his littermates was that, except for being cleaner and their coats better groomed, they looked exactly like a matted old tom cat who had roamed my neighborhood, cadged pets and solicited treats. Different neighbors looked after him but I heard stories about him from all over town. I figured he must have been Bits' dad, and the folks at the shelter told me that they had an awfully lot of little fluffy orange kittens. His—er—passion for procreation inspired Spam's family story and name.

Kittibits and I had a great life together for 16 years when he died from cancer. The last night before he died, he could barely walk and was sleeping with his head under the coffee table because the light hurt his eyes. I knew it was very near the end. I'd given him his fluids, he tottered back to lie down, and I came to the kitchen table to try to write. Then pretty soon he struggled to his feet, staggered into the kitchen, and sat down in front of me in the position that meant I was to pet him, especially on his head between his ears. I did. He managed a purr, and that was how he said goodbye to me because he didn't wake up again after that.

"That was not the end of our association, of course. He is my best mews when he visits my dreams or haunts the house on his frequent tours of inspection from the Rainbow Bridge."

Excerpt:
Spam Vs. the Vampire
by
Elizabeth Ann Scarborough
with
K. B. Dundee

Chapter 1

There was no indication when Darcy left the house that morning that she was going to get herself snatched by a vampire and wasn't coming back. She left our dishes half full, the litter box un-scooped, our fountains running, the TV set on the Critter Channel where we like it and the desk top computer on "sleep." If I had known what she was going to do, I'd have stopped her, even if it meant peeing on something vital or the ultimate sacrifice, acting sick enough for an emergency trip to the vet. But none of us had any idea she would just go away and *stay* away and none of us even thought to look for clues until the first day and night passed.

I, at least, was plenty anxious to see her. Even the night after she left, I ran from window to window, jumping onto the broad sills and looking out to try to see her coming. Usually I could hear her footsteps several minutes before she arrived but this time, she stubbornly continued not to appear.

When neither she nor anyone else showed up to open our cans, fill the kibble bowls or clean our trays, as one or two of her friends had done before when she was gone for more than one feeding, naturally everyone began to speculate. Except for the ones who were busy panicking.

"Okay," Rocky said, his half-tail jerking with agitation. "It's finally happened. Darcy's abandoned us, or else she's dead. Either way, we're finished. We've had it pretty good here but we're on our own again. Pretty soon the animal control van will come; we'll be hauled off to the so-called shelter and be forced to take the long dirt nap."

"That's if anyone even finds us before the food and water run out and we starve to death," BearPaws cried as if he had already started starving. Darcy had been gone long enough for us to miss two wet food meals by then and BearPaws was in mourning. He really loved his wet food.

"It's the storm," my mother said sensibly. "She must have got caught in it and hid somewhere till it let up."

"Don't be ridiculous, Board!" Max told her, raising his gray and white face from his paws. "Darcy's not like us. Humans don't get caught out in storms."

"Yes," said Cleo, who used to have a gift shop until the owner died and she came to live with Darcy. She's very sophisticated, Cleo is. "They go into shops and eating places and wait and talk with other humans. Often they buy things if you twine around their feet and act friendly. That gives them the chance to ask the clerk about you and the clerk a chance to ask them what they want to buy without seeming pushy."

"Are you suggesting she is neglecting us in order to go out and pet *other* cats?" my mother demanded.

"It happens," Trixie said. "You know it does. I've smelled her hands when she comes home after patting other cats. There's no getting around it. She's a sucker for a kitty face."

"Lucky for us," Max said. "That's why we're all here."

"The point is," Mother said, "We're here, but where is she?"

"Can't you find out from her 'puter, Spam?" my sister Bitbit asked.

"I don't think it tells you where people go," I said. "Anyway, we know that, don't we? She went out. Like she usually does."

"To pet *other* cats," Trixie said.

"Maybe, but she does it almost every day, sooner or later. She says she has to leave the house and see other humans. Yesterday she was going to meet that guy she's been building a website for."

"How do you know that?" my brother Byte asked.

"She said so. She said her client was going to pay her and she should be able to bring home treats." She didn't really say anything about treats but I thought it would make the others feel better if she had. And I was sure she *meant* to say that. Her good luck was always our good luck too. "Then she put her 'puter pad in her backpack and put that on over her outer coat, the black leather one, and walked across the street into the woods, like always. You all saw her. It was yesterday morning just before the storm started."

"Was he handsome? Maybe she stayed with him," Fat Mama suggested, sighing as she plopped down onto her belly. Fat Mama has had a lot of kittens in her day, most recently Coco, Mojo, Jojo and Cookie, who all live here too. All but Cookie are black, like Fat Mama.

Cookie is orange striped, like me and my brothers and sister, and half the cats in town, according to my mother. She told us our feral sire is an orange tabby. She says his hobby is making copies of himself.

"How would I know?" I asked.

Rocky jumped on his three good legs to the windowsill and peered out between the curtains. I'd been there off and on for the whole day too, watching the storm, listening to the wind as it moaned around the house, sometimes shaking it and making things rattle. It whipped the trees into a leafy hula dance and flattened the grass with the rain. Now it was almost dark again and the security light kept coming on, showing the depressingly empty yard.

"It's wild out there," Rocky said. "They were saying on the news that this is the worst storm since '76, when it lasted for six days. There are trees and power lines down all over the highway and the news dude said the bridge is closed. I'm guessing a tree bopped Darcy on the head and killed her outright."

Everybody started crying, me included. Rocky looked smug. Life sucked. He knew that and he was always glad when he was proved right, even if it meant our human mom might be dead and we'd all starve to death before anybody remembered about us.

"You and your news!" Mother said. "Why can't you watch the Critter Channel like the rest of us?"

"Because there's no bed to hide under in the living room, and Mojo and Coco are always playing under the couch is why," Fat Mama said. "Rocky's a big 'fraidy cat. That's why Darcy leaves on the TV in her bedroom for him, so he has company in the dark. You better hope the power doesn't go off, Mr. 'Fraidy Cat!"

"Darcy is *not* dead," Mother said firmly. "If she was, someone would come and take care of us."

"Unless they didn't *know* she was dead," Rocky said. "Coyotes might have got her."

Mother popped him one across the ear.

Darcy couldn't be dead. Dead was what Popsicle was when she laid all stiff and still on the rug in front of the stove, her fur getting cool and her scent—well, changing, and not in a good way. Dead was when you went to the vet and never came back again.

"I bet the tree knocked her out like one of those tranquilizer darts they use on TV," Trixie said. "She couldn't tell anyone to come and feed us,"

"Or a coyote got her," Rocky said.

"Coyotes don't get people. Only cats," Mother told him.

I left them arguing and returned to my place in the desk chair. When Darcy was here, she used the chair seat and I sat on the back and supervised, but I knew what was happening on the screen and although she didn't realize it, I know how to use the keypad too.

I may be a young cat who looks like most of the other young cats in town, but I have skills. And the laptop was still here. I am a whiz with the tablet that's her new portable because it responds easily to a paw touch but I've had more practice with the desktop. It's always on except when she goes to bed.

Darcy doesn't know I can use it but I practice every time she takes a break or goes away. Even though I'm only half grown, the other cats all know I am the one who helps her with her work and I know what I'm doing. Mom says I probably picked up my talent because she had me and my littermates in the gutted case of an old CPU. That's why Darcy named us all computer names—Mom is the mother *Board*, haha; and there's Bitbit, my sister; and Byte, Shifty, Alt and Escape, my brothers; but Darcy said she was darned if she was going to call me Delete. Since I looked so much like all the other kittens in town, she named me Spam.

She held me in her lap even before my eyes opened and I suckled, you might say, on the electronic impulse. When my eyes did open, instead of rough-housing with my littermates, I sat on her shoulder or lap or the back of her chair, or, when she wasn't looking, right beside the keyboard, watching and learning. She thought my brothers and I took turns sitting with her because she couldn't tell us apart then but nope, it was always me.

Of course I checked to see if the 'puter would tell me where she was. I tapped the news feed, but nope, no stories about cat owners getting bopped by trees.

I tapped on her projects in progress, a website for the grocery CO-OP where she gets our food, one for a local nursery and the "vampire dating site" she was creating for the guy from Montreal she called Marcel. He was the one she had been going to meet. Mew hoo! He even went to the library two or three times so he could video chat with her. It was always in the evening. She put on red lipstick before she talked to him and her voice changed. I gave her moral support by sitting on her lap. Her hands trembled when she petted me and I knew this was not just another client.

They did talk about work a little. He told her questions he wanted her to use to interview the prospects. I thought they were kind of odd. Especially the one about blood type. She laughed and said that would be the kind of question a vampire date would ask. He also wondered about family members living—or buried—near them and that sort of thing. Darcy told him she had no one, which wasn't true of course. She had us.

It was nice we had work, and I am all about getting kibble in the house, but I didn't like the look of this guy or the way Darcy acted when she was online with him.

She'd come here, I heard her telling her friend Perry, our sometimes-cat-sitter, to get away from a bad relationship. The male she'd been involved with had started taking drugs. I couldn't understand that. Drugs are the same thing as medicine like you get at the vet and why someone would take them on purpose is beyond me! But she said *her* habit had always been to pick guys who seemed nice but turned out to be mean, married or addicted to something so she had moved to Port Deception to get away from all that and from now on, the only males in her life would have tails and pointy ears.

I wanted to remind her of that when she talked to Marcel. He wasn't bad looking if you like human males, I suppose. All of his head fur was dark and kind of curly and his eyes were sort of hungry-looking. He had an oddly soothing voice—it almost put you to sleep, but I found him hard to understand. He didn't say his words the way Darcy did but she seemed to like the way he did it.

The last time they chatted, when they finished, she scooped me up and hugged me to her, kissing the top of my head. I learned long ago that resistance was futile, so I purred instead. "Maybe my luck with men has finally changed, Spammy. I think Marcel's really into me. Good thing for us he doesn't like the more public social networking sites and hired us instead. He's a private kinda guy, it sounds like. And hot. And—er—maybe rich?" She sighed, hugged and kissed me again, then tossed me to the floor and started her magic fingers flying across the keyboard. She checked a couple of accounts and winked at me. "The first $500 just hit my bank account. Just like that."

The next day she drove to the grocery store and returned with five bags of canned food and two thirty pound bags of kibble—plus canned salmon all around.

That was two weeks ago. I checked her mail trash and her send box and found an email from him saying, "I expect to be in Port Deception tomorrow night. Give me directions to your place."

But apparently her good sense kicked in then because she said, "I'd rather meet in the morning. Maybe at Bagels and Begonias Bakery?"

"Okay. I suppose I can find something to do in the meantime. I cannot wait to meet you," his email said. "But as it is a business meeting, for now, bring all of your work and your computer. Maybe you can give me a lesson?"

And that was the last entry. I wasn't sure what else to try. So I took a nap and waited some more.

The whole first night passed; and then a morning, and a long windy afternoon soon followed by the beginning of another wild windy night; and still Darcy didn't come home. The kibble dwindled to a sprinkling in the bottoms of the dishes and the water dispensers burbled the last of their wetness into the basins. Her scent wasn't nearly as strong in the chair or on the keyboard as it had been. I rubbed my face against the keys and tried to nap but kept waking up and jumping onto the windowsill long after the other cats had settled down to sleep. Rocky passed the office door.

"Get used to it, kit. She's not coming back. You were born in captivity. You haven't been out in the world and learned what humans are really like yet."

"Rocky, she has never been anything but nice to you and all the others. If you had been born here like I was, you'd know it's not captivity, it's how cats and their people are supposed to be."

He gave a little growl and limped away.

I huddled against the cool windowpane after that, watching the wind blow and waiting for the jingle of her house keys in her hand as she approached the kitchen door.

I was so sad I was almost convinced I'd never hear that sound again when I did. The house keys. There they were. The clink of keys tapping together, a smaller sound but very distinct against the wind.

But there was something wrong. I'd heard no footsteps. The security light hadn't gone on and though I peered back toward the kitchen door, I couldn't see Darcy.

Barking exploded from next door. Angry, loud barking so scary I flew off the windowsill as if someone had shot me.

A key clicked in the kitchen door. Well, I hadn't seen her but it had to be Darcy. Didn't it? Or maybe Perry, come to cat sit since Darcy was gone. I had to see anyway. I sprinted to the office door.

The kitchen door creaked then slammed open with the wind. My mother and littermates, who usually sleep under the kitchen table, streaked past me in a blur of fur. Other drowsy heads snapped up and the living room, where some of my housemates had been dozing, was suddenly catless.

Who could it be? I slunk toward the kitchen, ears flat and whiskers quivering. I did not smell Darcy, not unless Rocky was right and she was dead. The wind drove the scent through the kitchen and into me. None of it was anything *like* Darcy.

The dog barking up a storm in the middle of the storm, that was familiar too. Had it been just last night when I was aroused from my nap on Darcy's pillow by Darcy rousing from *her* pillow and looking out the window? The dog was barking then too, and there was the same rotten stench and something flapping outside our window—at its center was a bright white oval face with red glowing eyes.

I crept toward the kitchen, my curiosity strengthened by the memory. The dead something had flown into the night, and Darcy lay down again, sleeping as if she had never come all the way awake, and nothing unusual had happened. After awhile, I did too. End of close encounter of the weird kind.

Before I reached the door, somebody sneezed. I heard two footsteps and then even more violent sneezing. I slunk toward the door between the living room and the kitchen, peered around the frame into the darkened kitchen. The door was wide open, shadows dancing through and the wind billowing something black into the room. I hissed without meaning to and the sneezing got even louder. The darkness and the billowing blackness suddenly withdrew as if they'd been sucked out of the room, and the door slammed shut.

Drat! I had missed my chance. I could have raced out past whoever or whatever it was and gone to look for Darcy to get her to come home.

"Is it gone?" Fat Mama asked, her eyes shining huge as she peeped out from behind the trash can. "I like to wet myself when that thing came in. Good thing it's allergic to cats."

"It is?"

"What you think all that sneezing was about, Spam? That was a burglar was what that was. Musta stole Darcy's keys when she got hit by the tree—"

"Or eaten by the coyote," Rocky put in helpfully from the living room.

"And came to steal her stuff but he's too allergic to us to even come in the house."

"Good thing she's got us guard cats," Alt said, stalking past me with his chest puffed out, like he hadn't just come from under the bed.

"Can you call 911 on the 'puter, Spam?" Cookie asked me.

"I already pushed the 'help' menu. It gave me a whole lot of other menus, but none of them said anything about getting someone to find Darcy or come and feed us. I'm pretty sure it wouldn't say anything about burglars who are allergic to cats either."

"But that's not what you do," Max said. "You don't push a help button. You call 911. That's what people do on TV."

"Darcy took her phone with her," I told him. We don't have a phone with wires. Just the one Darcy carries with her.

"Keep trying to find someone to help us on the 'puter, dear," Mother said. "From what you say, there are lots of people in there if you just know how to find them. You have to sit very still, you know. Perhaps you're lashing your tail too much?"

I started to tell her it didn't work that way when Rocky broke in, "Face it, cats, you don't really want anyone else to come. Those animal cops on TV look all kind and concerned and stuff but in real life they snatch you, put you in a cell with a little food and water and a tiny little litter tray until it's time for them to gas you. Not even you kittens are still cute enough to get adopted. It never happens. Trust me on this."

"You talk like you know, but you got out," Max said.

"I used to be pretty fast, back when I had all four paws," Rocky said, sitting down and giving special attention to the claws of his right front foot.

"Find Perry," Mother said. She really likes Perry best of any of our cat-sitters. "Perry will come and help us and find Darcy too. She lives in the 'puter too, doesn't she?"

I didn't answer that time, just jumped back into my chair and tried to look busy until they stopped paying attention. I didn't want to admit that I didn't know how to get the people who were inside the 'puter to actually come out and talk to me.

I watched the screen until it went dark, then tapped the bar with my paw and made it light up again and watched it some more. Finally I fell asleep. Well, I might have done it more than once.

It was still early in the day because it hadn't got dark yet, even with the wind and rain, when our territory was breached again. This time there was no key, just the clatter of glass sending everyone ducking for cover. There was no sneezing either. Just the glass and then the tromp of heavy men feet as two guys stomped straight past our empty dishes in the kitchen and through the living room and—yikes! Into the office. I ducked beneath the desk as they unplugged the laptop from the big monitor. Our last link with the outside world and they were swiping it!

I wanted to cry but they were very large and scary, and I was afraid.

Then they did something that made me feel much better. They stuck the 'puter in a big cloth bag and stomped into Darcy's bedroom and opened drawers and pulled out clothes and went to the bathroom and took stuff out of there—I couldn't see what but I heard stuff being tossed into the bag.

Maybe these were just very crude friends taking her stuff to the hospital, where she had gone after the tree fell on her (or the coyote tried to eat her). Or a car hit her, maybe, or she got sick. Anyway, they were taking not just the computer but personal items with her scent all over them, things that were not valuable but would be useful to Darcy, who had to still be alive!

Maybe it would be worth a meow? But no, these could not be friends who came to help her. They stomped right past all of the faces they didn't see under the furniture and back past the empty food dishes. That was the giveaway. If these were Darcy's friends, and they were acting for her because she was hurt, they would have filled the kibble dishes, filled the water dispensers, and opened a few cans from the cupboards besides. Darcy would have definitely said "feed the cats" before she said, "bring me clean clothes and my toothbrush." I was sure of that. When Rocky came to us after he lost his leg, she didn't bathe or change her clothes or brush her teeth until she was sure he was going to be okay— but she did feed the rest of us.

I knew what I had to do. I shot past the big feet out into the windy yard before the men even noticed there'd been a cat there! I would follow them and I would find Darcy. That's what I would do. And we'd all be saved.

♥ ♥ ♥ ♥

Darcy opened her eyes. It was dark, the world was rocking and swaying like a farmhouse caught in a tornado, and her head hurt terribly. One minute it had been morning and she'd been walking through the woods, the trees surrounding her writhing in the gale blowing in off the Strait. The next thing she knew she was here, wherever here was. She thought she might have been hit by a tree blown down by the wind, but had somehow missed the part where the tree actually smacked her in the head. In almost every windstorm there were reports of trees taking out cars, houses and people. It must have been her turn.

"Hello, Darcy," a man's voice said from behind her. She turned to look and instantly the pain made her wish she hadn't.

"Hi?" she said, her voice weak and trembly. "That must have been some tree!" She rubbed the back of her head. "Ouch."

"Tree?"

"The tree that fell on me. Gosh, I wish I could enjoy saying this more since I've always wanted the chance but—who are you? Where am I?"

He came from the shadows cast by the single LED lantern rocking back and forth overhead, casting shadows like dancing cannibals. "It's me, Darcy. Don't you recognize me? Marcel, your client from Montreal? By chance I was coming to see you when I found you lying in the woods. My—friends—and I brought you back here to their boat."

A boat. That explained the rocking and bouncing, but there was something else wrong with this picture. She couldn't see Marcel very well but he didn't look like she'd imagined him—or much like the pictures he'd sent. That wasn't unusual of course. A lot of people on dating sites put up pictures either heavily doctored or of someone better looking. He didn't seem to be that bad looking, actually, just different. "Uh, thanks, I guess. You could have just dropped me at home."

"Hardly! You may have a concussion. You should not be alone."

"Everything is a little fuzzy," she admitted. "Did you decide to come and find me when I didn't show up for our appointment at the bakery?"

"Ah yes, the bakery, where we were supposed to meet this morning. You see? You should have met me last night as I wished and you would have avoided the bump on the head! I am not really a morning person. But yes, when you didn't come to the bakery, I became alarmed and took the shortcut through the woods to your house. I phoned my friends to come and help me bring you here to rest. You were unconscious."

"I guess so," she admitted. "What time is it?"

"Perhaps eight o'clock in the evening."

"I really have to get home."

"Not yet. Rest for awhile," he said. "We should talk." He looked deeply into her eyes and seemed so compassionate, so caring, that even though she knew it was a really bad idea for many reasons, not the least of which was that the cats would be wanting their din-din, she couldn't stop looking at him.

"Okay," she said, rolling onto her side and trying to look casual as he paced back and forth by the bed. There was something really wrong with this picture other than the time she seemed to have lost and the difference in his looks. He was scarily intense and she tried to defuse the situation. "What made you decide to move out here, or to the States, Marcel? I know you said you planned to move here eventually but I didn't realize you meant here to Port Deception. Won't it seem kind of provincial after life in the big city?"

"Not at all. I am weary of the city and all my responsibilities. So I retired from my position, and came to a new place, where no one knows me. Except you." Another long look.

"But a vampire dating site?" she asked. "That's not going to be everybody's bag."

He smiled at her, a half smile. "No, but it's me. And it is chic now to be a vampire, especially here. And so I have come to this place to enjoy life." The last part sounded oddly ironic. "So now, my dear friend, you should rest. Sleep. It will do you good."

She didn't want to rest there. She wanted to go home. But when she tried to swing her legs over the side of the wedge-shaped bed, she found she couldn't. She was so sleepy. Very sleepy. She drifted off again.

To be awakened by Marcel demanding, "Why didn't you tell me you had a house full of cats?"

"Didn't I mention?" she asked. That was unusual. With some people all she did was talk about the cats but she had found it put some men off, even as clients, so unless they mentioned pets, she tried not to discuss hers. Marcel was usually quite willing to do most of the talking anyway.

She had thought he was cute when he first contacted her and they started chatting. His anger now scared her. She didn't know him. He could be some kind of nut or something. She certainly was, to get into this position where she was alone with him in the little boat with no one except his "friends" knowing she was there.

When he stepped into the lantern light, she saw that his pale skin was covered with a bright red rash.

"I am very allergic to them, cats," he said. "How can you bear to have them creeping around you?"

"I love them," she said. Normally she would have said more than that. In fact, normally she would have sent any guy who objected to her cats packing, but since she was in his space that wasn't an option.

She sat up and swung her legs over the edge of the bed. She settled for, "What were you doing at my place, anyway?"

"I was going to get you some of your things, and your computer. You did not bring it. I asked you to bring it."

"I don't need my things. I need to go home," she said firmly.

"I paid you well to do a job," he said.

"Nowhere in our contract did it say that you get to drag me off to a boat somewhere until you're satisfied," she said. He didn't even protest this time that he had found her lying on the path, which told her, as she had to admit to herself that she already suspected, that he was the headache behind her headache. "And I did bring my computer. I copied everything onto the iPad." She stood up, her head swimming a little. This was not helped when the boat took another wild swing in the wind and threatened to throw her back onto the bed. She resolutely clutched the wall instead. "If I can find my pack, I'll show you," and she brushed past him into the narrow corridor with a door that probably contained the toilet and on out into a room boasting a long padded red plush sofa on one side and booth with a Formica table top in boomerang patterns and leopard print covered benches.

Her purple pack was on the floor, no doubt thrown there by a heave of the hull. Holding onto the table, she bent over and retrieved it. When she stood again, he was in her face. His breath made the cats' mouse-breath sweet by comparison. She saw what she was pretty sure was blood caked at the edge of his lips. "Look here," she said, sidestepping him to slide into one of the booths and pull the tablet out of its case.

She concentrated on the familiar device to keep from panicking, and tried to interest him in it too. But for someone who had paid so much for a website, he wasn't paying much attention to it. "Where are the dates?" he asked. "The women who are hot for vampires?"

"They have to find your site," she said. Geez, this guy was serious about the whole vampire thing. "You could log on to one of the vamp movie fan sites maybe, and include a link to your site. Or get a Facebook profile."

"Yes," he said, "Do that. But how do we get the women here to see it?"

"Um—it's a small town really, Marcel. I'm not sure the website will be much help. If we'd met at the bakery, I could have introduced you around."

He gave her a disgusted look followed by a fangy Halloween grin, and shook his head. "I don't do days."

"Oh, yeah, well that is a problem. They roll up the sidewalks early here." she said, but she was muttering. Either this guy had a really good pros-thetic dentist or he was, as he claimed, the real thing. Either way, she was probably dead. She felt the hairs rise at the nape of her neck and up and down her arms. Like the cats, she thought. Oh, poor cats. Poor dumb women who might be lured in by her website. If she lived long enough, she was going to be an accessory to murder, from the looks of things.

Instead of looking at what she was trying to show him on the website, he snatched the tablet away from her, sweeping it from the table. Before she could retrieve it he took her hands in his. His were cold and a little clammy. "Pay close attention," he said, and she thought he was going to tell her something. But he just stared into her eyes until all she could see was his eyes. She wanted to scream or bolt from the cabin of the boat. There were people around all the time, people who lived on their boats. Someone would hear her. Someone would help her. But the idea seemed to slip from her mind. Her arms and legs would not move and she could not look away from his eyes. As surely as if she were duct taped in place, she could not escape. Her last conscious thought before she drowned in the depths of his eyes was that if only she had known this sort of thing was likely to happen, she would have called someone to look after the cats.

Vampires on the Olympic Peninsula:

Everybody knows about those sparkly vampires over by Forks, about a hundred miles west of where we live.

The idea for the plot of this story came to me when a local woman, one I knew slightly and often shared morning coffee with at the old Bread and Roses Bakery with a group of assorted characters, disappeared. Like many people who disappear in the US, she never was found. She lived with another person and the circumstances of her disappearance were extremely indicative that hers was not a voluntary leave-taking. Being somewhat cat-centric, I thought, *what if she had been the sole support of a house full of cats and disappeared without knowing she was going to? The cats might easily starve to death before anyone even realized she was missing, since they couldn't report her absence.* That was the germ of the idea. Halfway through writing it though, I stumbled against the certainty that the missing woman probably would have fallen prey to one of the serial killers of women like the Green River Killer (though the victim was *not* a prostitute, as many of the GRK's victims were). Something about the gloom and rain and probably good digging conditions in the woods in the Pacific Northwest seems to attract that kind criminal. I didn't want to go into grisly sex-and-torture killings, but was stumped for a motive other-wise. Then it occurred to me that vampires often keep their victims alive for a number of much-storified and gorified vampiric reasons. And the rea-son the vampire did not remain with his intended *bride* in her own home was simple—he was allergic to the cats.

Garlic, crosses, silver, cats—who knew?

COMING SOON:
SPAM AND THE TOUR BUS OF DOOM
Elizabeth Ann Scarborough
with
K.B. Dundee

First came the vampires. After all the movies promoting our neck of the woods (or the Olympic National Forest, to be exact) as ideal for the undead, out of town vampires arrived. I helped deport some of them, since they were Canadian but even I'll admit *Spam, Vampire Deporter* just doesn't have the sound bite—pardon the expression—that *Slayer* does.

When the tour bus of doom pulled up in front of Elevated Ice Cream, I felt no sense of dread or foreboding but instead hightailed it to my favorite bench on the back deck. Some of my best friends are tourists. Travelers lonely for their cats at home bribe me with whipped cream and melted ice cream, hoping to cop a pet. Unless they are very young and their hands are very sticky, I graciously oblige. I love imagining the frenzied rubbing and marking the tourists are in for when they return home and their feline housemates get a whiff of Spam.

I've made lots of new friends recently. For a while, after the whole vampire thing, I was worried about our human mom, Darcy; but she needed me less than I thought she would. In fact, since I rescued her, once she recovered from the shock, she started working really hard to make up for the money she lost while she was out of commission— pardon the expression again! On top of that, she started hanging out with, of all people, Deputy Shelter Dude, the sheriff's deputy who takes care of the shelter! That made all of us cats nervous, especially Rocky, though now that he is a catpire (or vampcat, if you prefer) he sleeps in the cupboard most of the day so isn't too aware of what happens then.

The first time DSD (okay, his name is Daryl) was still there when the sun went down, Rocky took one look at him—no, one sniff—and rocketed out the cat flap, to which only he and I have keys. Maddog, who seems to be sort of Vampire Law and Order Officer South of the (Canadian) Border, installed my private entrance after he helped me rescue Darcy. He recognized the kind of cat I am and that Rocky, trying to defend our house, became a bloodsucker too. Darcy hadn't figured out that Maddog and Rocky were both vampires, which was a good thing because after her last experience, she was sick of them. But even she realized that I am no ordinary housecat.

Having had a taste of the great outdoors, where I made quite a few new friends, I had no desire to return to being housebound, even to oversee the office. I became an unusual creature in Port Deception, an outdoor cat. Not a stray, not feral, and not lunch for coyotes, thanks to Rocky's new hunting habits as Vampcat the Coyote Slayer, but an *emancipated* cat, with my own entry to my house and the freedom to come and go as I wished.

In the long bright hours of summer when the grass smelled sweet and the light sea breeze kept my fur coat from being too hot for comfort, I definitely wished to be out. Not only was there my network of four-legged friends-who-were—not-cats to maintain, I had on my previous expeditions encountered several of my half brothers and sisters, and I wanted to deepen my family ties.

For a cat with a wide ranging if transitory territory, having as many siblings who might be prevailed upon to share a napping spot and a food dish when said cat grew footsore and hungry was a good thing. Besides, seeing my lookalike half brothers and sisters gave me a sense of what my life could have been like. Not that I wanted to trade. I was just, you know, curious.

Most of them fared pretty well, as gorgeous orange tabby cats such as ourselves are apt to do, but Marigold, the last one on my rounds tonight, had been so upset I could hear her cry from the street. I don't have that many lookalike sisters as for some strange reason cats of our coloring tend to be male. But Marigold looked just like my brothers and me, except for the girly bits. If it hadn't been for me, she wouldn't be alive now. I'd met her and her mother right after she was born at Christmas and kept the owls and coyotes off them till they were rescued by humans and eventually found nice homes. Deputy Daryl told Darcy it was love at first site between Marigold and her little human girl, Amy, less of a cat mom and more of a kitten-sister.

"What's the matter, little sis?" I asked through the mail slot. "Is someone standing on your tail?"

"Nooo, but my family's gone and left me and I don't think I'll ever see them again," she cried. "They've been gone so long and I tell you, bro, I've got a terrible feeling about this."

"They covered the important parts though, didn't they? Someone comes to feed you and change your box?"

"It doesn't matter! They've been gone weeks and weeks. Even the sitter says they've been gone a lot longer than she agreed to take care of me. Not that she'll stop. She adores me, naturally. But I want my own people back. NYOW!"

"You said they went on vacation, a cruise to some island somewhere?"

"They would not leave me to go play. They are on an important relief mission to help hurricane victims on some wretched island. I am very proud of them, though understandably annoyed by the inconvenience and abandonment."

I really felt I should do something about it, but there was a mail slot between us. "If I could come in, I would show you how to work the computer," I told her. "Then you could maybe go online and find them, since you can't get out."

"I know how to use the computer," she said. "I've played video games till I have carpaw tunnel syndrome."

"I am *Spamnotthebadkind@moggyblog.com,*" I told her. "Let me know if they show up." I know how upsetting it can be to be abandoned by your human.

Since I couldn't make her feel better, I decided to try instead to make me feel better and proceeded down the hill and into downtown, making a sharp left at the second intersection, pitter-patting across the street and walking boldly into the ice cream store.

My friend Amanda had the counter alone that night, while Eric the ice cream maker worked in the back. Elevated Ice Cream is the best place in town for a nocturnal critter like me, since they are open till ten and people come in from the movies and ball games to get goodies afterward.

Even so, on week nights when there is no game at Memorial Field, town is mostly quiet as the evening rolls on. You could hear the bugs buzzing the street lights. How I wished I could reach them! A few people still wandered the sidewalks, but not a soul sat in the red plastic booths or the patio chairs set around little tables in the back.

Nevertheless, I was not allowed to remain on the premises. Amanda and I had worked out a deal. I meowed to let her know I was ready to be served. She came around the counter and knelt down to give me a couple of pets, held my face in her hands and looked into my eyes, "Your usual, sir?"

"Meow," I said, affirmatively.

"Okay. Go out and sit down. I'll be there in a minute."

I trotted back to the deck and stretched out on one of the tables to wait for my server to deliver my ice cream.

The waves slapped pleasantly against the shore beneath the roofed viewing gallery stretched the length of the parking lot. Delicious smells came from the Mexican restaurant across the street. Unfortunately, they were closed now, or I would have gone over and made myself irresistible. I could almost taste the seafood in the chimichanga.

A pirate strode down the sidewalk on the opposite side of the street. This week was the Kinetic Sculpture Race, and many of the humans put on colorful costumes. Some humans even made their animal friends wear costumes. Some animal friends didn't even mind. I wasn't one of those, so I was glad Darcy had figured out that none of the cats who lived at our house would take kindly to being swathed, buckled, velcroed or pinned into silly outfits that would hide our beautiful natural coats.

Amanda duly brought out my spoonful of ice cream in the plastic lid to a takeout cup. I licked her fingers then licked my ice cream. She ran her hand from my ears to my tail and gave me a squeeze. I ignored it. Now was the time for ice cream. Petting came later. She sighed heavily and went back inside.

I was taking my final lick when I heard the bus rumbling down the street. Cars are not unusual at this time of night, but busses? Sometimes an RV will go by, heading for the campgrounds at the beach. But this had the distinct sound of a bus. Finishing my ice cream, I jumped down, ran through the parking lot to the front sidewalk and hid under the bench to scope things out.

Something was wrong with this picture, I thought, watching the big vehicle roll up the street toward me. I had never seen a tour bus arrive so late, looking so dark, silent, and blind. The front of the bus was dark where headlights ought to shine. Of course, the street lights were bright enough to see by, but still . . .

The bus pulled up outside the ice cream store just as Amanda turned out the light. The door hissed open and a man in a Hawaiian shirt, camouflage cargo shorts, and running shoes with no socks got out.

Well, that explained the wrong part, I thought, sniffing more than I'd intended. The dude was dead, and he wasn't the only one. There was a lot of dead there. I'm even more of an authority on dead than most cats, having recently had a close encounter of the weird kind with vampires—well, mostly one. This bus dude was different though. On a scale of deadness, he was a ten to the vampire's five.

For one thing, he'd lost his hair. He wasn't just bald. He didn't have anything on top of his skull, at all. For just a nanosecond I watched him, fascinated, expecting the rest of his face to slip down to his neck without the scalp to hold it up.

Lots of cats like dead things, but this did not look or smell edible. Not remotely. Not to me anyway.

The thing shuffled toward the ice cream store's door. Amanda looked up and said, "Wow, great costume!" then caught a whiff of his aroma. "Holy crap, dude, you can't come in here smelling like that!"

She was around the counter and at the door, where she got the full benefit of his perfume. Holding her nose, she slammed the door in his face. "Sorry, closed."

The smelly guy reared back his fist to send it through the window, but a very spooky riff on a hand drum of some sort (there's an African drumming group that plays sometimes near my favorite pizzeria, so I know about drums) stopped him—er—dead—in his tracks.

He backed up and stood beside the open bus door. Two more figures descended the steps with slow, stomping movements while the drum thumped a slow, stomping beat.

A dazed-looking barefooted lady wearing shorts and a halter top almost fell onto the sidewalk. She didn't seem to have any bits falling off her, though her short blonde hair stuck up at all angles, like someone had scared her. Behind her, a man also in shorts and a t-shirt climbed out of the darkened bus onto the lamplit sidewalk. He was wearing sunglasses, which seemed kind of weird.

These two were fragrant too, but in the delicious way people get when they haven't unnaturally removed all their scents by taking showers and such. Their scents were very strong . Behind these people came two young girls, maybe ten or eleven years old—I have a hard time telling with human kittens. Their eyes were open and staring, like the older ones. As they walked stiff-legged from the bus, the drums picked up in tempo. The young ones sort of quickstepped forward until they had their noses pressed against the window of the ice cream store.

This was all very interesting, but I wasn't sure it was in my best interests to stick around. These did not look like normal tourists, even during Kinetic Sculpture season.

I slunk along the wall behind the bench and around it while more dead passengers got off the bus. Behind the wall was the parking lot leading to the deck in the back of the store and more parking lot. I wasn't even there yet when I heard Amanda saying, "It was a zombie, Eric, I swear it! Totally disgusting . . ." She paused and the thump and pat of the drum pounced in from the street. "Great music, though."

"Maybe it was a Halloween group, dying for ice cream?" Eric asked in his calm way. He had a dry sense of humor, I'd noticed before. When he gave me ice cream, he always apologized for not having any raspberry rodent flavor.

"In stinkovision?" Amanda asked. I met them on the deck, near the back door. "Let's just *go.*"

I mewed and pawed Eric's leg to tell him she had the right idea.

She glanced down at that and scooped me up. "Come on, kitty, you can't stay here. I'll take you— shit."

" What's the matter?" Eric asked.

"I rode my bike. I don't think that's very good for getting away from zombies."

"Well, but they're probably not zombies," Eric said. "Though just in case I guess I'd better see if I can come up with brain-flavored ice cream."

"Yuck!" she said.

I squirmed for her to let me down. I appreciated the offer of protection, but I could hide under things she and her bike couldn't; and I didn't want to lose that advantage. Besides, I wanted to see what happened next. I intended to keep these people under surveillance. I'm a cat. I'm curious. So sue me.

In the Joe Grey detective books, Joe, Dulcey and Kit hop from rooftop to rooftop in their little California town. The architects of Port Deception weren't that considerate of feline operational needs. The buildings are all different sizes. The older Victorian ones are usually two or three stories, but there are some newer places that only have one story, which is a long jump even for a cat with a superior gyroscope in his back end, such as my fluffy orange tabby tail.

I circled around the former police station and rejoined the sidewalk half a block down from the bus. No one was in front of it now. Oh no! What if the zombies had heard us talking and shambled back in the parking lot to munch on Amanda and Eric? There wasn't a whole lot I could do about it and besides, shouldn't there be screams if that was happening? I stopped worrying when suddenly an

Amanda-laden bike zipped out of the ice cream store parking lot and whizzed down the street in front of me. Looked like my pal had made a clean getaway. Then a battered older truck that used to be orange, maybe, pulled out of the lot and followed the bike. That would be Eric. Good. The innocent bystanders were being removed from the scene, lessening possible collateral damage. I was an innocent bystander too, of course, being a young cat with a network of siblings to think of, not to mention monitoring the activities of Rocky, the gleeful coyote-munching cat-pire; and Renfrew, my raccoon assistant detective who worked for kibble.

I really should hop in the back of that truck and snag a ride up the hill toward my house, away from the downtown dead.

But you know, there was something familiar about that second set of zombies that got out of the bus, the man and woman and kids. For spooky scary types, they looked like they belonged in Port Deception.

I crossed the dark and mostly quiet road to the other side, heading in the opposite direction from my fleeing friends.

The drumming grew louder as I ran down the street. Of course, my pointy ears are very sensitive, but the drums didn't seem to be making music so much as a one-sided conversation. In the time it took me to cross the street and jump onto the patio roof of the Gooseberry Cafe and from there onto the slightly higher roof of the shop with the magical rocks and the elephant god in the window, a whole bus load of zombies jerked, shuffled, and danced their way down the street, crossed at the crosswalk, lured on by the pat-a-pats and hollow thumps on the drum.

Port Deception doesn't have a huge business district. There are only about four blocks of Water Street, so it was no problem seeing where the zombies went. Even if I hadn't been able to see in the dark, I could see them lurching and sometimes dropping pieces of themselves onto the sidewalk. *Mewww.*

The drum changed its tune slightly and half the zombies broke off—well, not literally. I mean, they separated into two groups. One of the groups left the rest of the pack and crossed the street to the side I was on. On my side of that block were a couple of gift stores and the bank; on the other side, nothing much aside from one big gift shop, a half-empty gallery, and a closed diner.

Something heavy shattered glass and my poor little pointy ears were attacked by a screaming siren. Unconcerned, zombies shuffled into the bank and back out again. I guess banks don't leave all their money lying around at night. One zombie did come out with a nice chair and used it to break the glass in the insurance office on the next block.

It got very noisy there, and I jumped back down off the roof onto the roof of the cafe across the street from the bank parking lot. The zombies didn't seem to be searching for cats, so I figured as long as I kept off the main street and up high, I could see what was going on. Between the bank and the gift store next door was a little patch of greenery, including a biggish tree. I climbed it, hoping I'd remember how I got down from the last one I climbed. All I remembered about it at the moment was that it wasn't easy.

Once I got to the top of the tree, I saw that I could jump across onto the bank's roof and watch zombies break into the bookstore, the diner, three gift shops, the used book shop, and the jeweler's. The front of the jewelry store was not quite as dark as the others. Some did keep lights on in their windows, but I happened to know that the jeweler, who liked cats, often went in late at night to work.

The noises of alarm bells and shattering glass were joined by a third loud, scary noise—a gunshot. I cringed against the flat asphalt bank roof. Two more shots and gruff shouts of, "Get out of here, you . . ." and the voice broke off in gurgle. The drums stopped too. Peering way over the edge, I saw Mr. Jeweler Dude meeting the drummer and the two of them disappeared into his shop. Pretty soon zombies came out carrying all kinds of stuff, and Mr. Jeweler did too. Some of the lady zombies had new purses with cats on them from the store next to the bookstore. None of them had stolen any books though. They all shambled back up the street toward the bus.

The police must have been busy fighting crime elsewhere, because the zombies were already back on the bus by the time the first cop car arrived. The bus just drove away at a normal pace and the cops didn't even try to stop it. They were busy looking at the broken glass.

I was bored now and jumped back into the tree, jumping from one branch to another until I was within a short distance from the ground. I landed on soft grass and looked around the corner. No zombies; just cops and a single furry blur with a shiny bit in the middle.

I knew that blur. "Pssst, Renfrew!" I called to the raccoon who served as my assistant detective. "What did you find?"

"Never you mind, housecat. This shiny thing is mine, and you are not going to make me give it to anybody else."

"You sure do hold a grudge," I said, as he drew nearer. "Come on, let me see. I don't want it but I'm a cat and, you know, inquisitive."

He rolled it from one front paw to the other, bit it, pulled it out from between his teeth and examined it. "That's gold all right! I found gold in the middle of the sidewalk."

I started to say that one of the zombies probably dropped it when they were looting the jewelry store, but I figured Renfrew would worry I'd try to make him give it back. Maybe I would have, if the jeweler dude was still around, but he had been dancing to the zombie drums the last time I saw him.

"So it's gold!" I snapped. Sometimes raccoons can be very shallow. "So what? What are you going to do with it? Invest it?"

"Not until I wash it again," he said. "Washing makes it shinier."

"And then?"

"When it gets dull, I'll wash it again."

"The zombies might want it back. I think it belongs to Mr. Stone, the jeweler dude, and he's a zombie now."

"How could you tell?" he asked.

"I saw it happen," I told him. "Before the tour bus of doom full of zombies drove off again."

"I think you've been getting some of that tainted cat food, Spam. Took a nap and woke up with nightmares."

"Maybe," I said. "But I don't think so."

"Sure you did. Let's go back to your house and get some kibble. That will make you feel better."

I saw right through his concern for *my* health, of course, but going home was a good idea so we set off up the hill toward home. The walk is a fairly long one for cat and coon legs, but not as long as I once thought, before I knew the way. Heading straight up the hill to the uptown area, all we had to do was turn left onto Blair Street until we found the trail leading through the woods to the street in front of my house. Renfrew, carrying his new treasure between his teeth, had a little trouble keeping up, so I was the first one to see the damage to Blair street. The huge front window at the corner grocery where the shed boys had coffee lay in glittering pieces under the lamplight, amid piles of ruined food.

This got Renfrew's immediate attention, and he dropped the coin to graze in the spoiling inventory. Smelling only the residue of zombie stink, I followed him in, dodging broken glass. Not only the window, but everything that came in bottles and jars lay broken on the floor and sidewalk. What looked like a mess of eyeballs turned out to be spilled olives . Apparently zombies don't like them. Beer was another matter. A cooler surrounded by puddles of it and more smashed glass was pretty much empty.

Zombies liked beer? Who knew?

Something else they liked was meat. The meat counter was torn to splinters and the walk-in freezer door was wrenched off its hinges so the steamy cold filled the air like zombie breath.

"Come on, Renfrew," I said, shivering. "Let's get out of here. This place gives me the creeps."

A head of cabbage with raccoon ears looked up from the produce counter and mumbled.

"What?"

"You go ahead," Renfrew said through a full mouth. "I'll just stay here and help clean up the mess."

"How about the kibble at home?"

"I'm not hungry right now," Renfrew said. "But save me some!"

"Right!" I said, trying to sound disgusted; but the truth was, I didn't really like the idea of going into the woods on my own. I left the store and passed the health food store, which had also been trashed and the bar, and the video store. I didn't go in there, but I was willing to bet the zombie movies and games were missing.

A police car with its sirens blaring roared up the hill behind me and I scampered down the street until I reached the path, and ten bolted up it. I wasn't afraid of the police car, but it hurt my ears.

Once I was in the woods though, alone, in the woods where bigger animals than housecats live, at night, with zombies prowling the town, the police car noise stopped and was replaced by the cries of nightbirds, including the hoots of owls. Owls were fond of having cats for late night suppers. They just

85

swooped down on you, silently, and you didn't know what hit you until suddenly you were up in the air suspended from a cruel beak and claws.

What were zombies, compared to that? I hadn't seen any movies where zombies attacked cats, come to think of it. In the movies—not that we watched a lot of them—but sometimes Darcy left the TV on when she fell asleep and one would come on. They apparently fed on humans. Possibly they did not like fur between their teeth, although they didn't look all that fastidious.

Owls didn't mind fur. Coyotes didn't either. The wind picked up as it often seems to do in the evening, and the trees rustled, sounding a little crackly, since the leaves were already turning colors, dying and becoming crisp and brittle.

I trotted up the path, waving my tail like I was not a bit spooked to walk in the woods where there were mountain lions, coyotes and owls, oh my.

Shiny eyes stared at me from the sides of the path as I walked up it. "Hi, there," I said. "Lovely evening we're having." Eyes blinked out as the owner returned to his or her own business. I wasn't alarmed. I could pretty well smell who was there. A coon, a possum, a deer family of four, another coon, another possum, a couple of feral cats who skittered into the bushes after we exchanged territorial glares.

Then I smelled the wild doggy scent of coyote. No eyes, just stink. *Climb a tree, climb a tree,* I told myself. I sprang for the nearest trunk and leaped up, holding on with all four sets of pitons.

The stupid tree didn't have any branches low enough for me to jump onto. *Climb another tree! Climb another tree!* I told myself. But then the coyote was at the bottom of the trunk, grinning up at me with his sharp canine teeth.

"Hel-LO, midnight snack," she said. With a sniffer like mine, you can tell about gender, not that it mattered.

I didn't reply. My mom always said not to talk to strange coyotes.

"What's the matter, kitty kitty? Cat got your tongue?" She laughed and laughed and it turned into a yip and howl. For my part, I yowled at the top of my lungs. "Bubba!" I cried, calling the retired police dog who lives next door to us. Not that he'd come. He was probably in the house asleep with his partner. "Renfrew! Rocky! Deer! Anybody! I could use a little help here."

The coyote leapt, and I felt her hot breath under the hairs of my tail. She fell back, gathering herself to try again.

One more leap and she would grab my poor tail and that would be the end of it, if not me.

Bibliography

By Elizabeth Scarborough and/or Elizabeth Ann Scarborough

Songs of the Seashell Archives

1.Song of Sorcery—Bantam 1982 (eBook 2009 E-Reads (ER))
2.The Unicorn Creed Bantam 1983 (eBook 2010 Gypsy Shadow Publishing (GSP))
3.Bronwyn's Bane—Bantam 1984 (eBook 2010 GSP)
4.Christening Quest—Bantam 1986 (eBook 2010 GSP)

(stand-alone)
5.The Harem of Aman Akbar—Bantam 1985 (eBook 2010 GSP)

V. Lovelace's Guide to the Wild West duo
6. The Drastic Dragon of Draco, Texas—Bantam, 1986 (eBook 2010 GSP)
7. The Goldcamp Vampire—Bantam, 1987 (eBook 2010 GSP)

(stand-alone)
8.*The Healer's War—Bantam, 1989 Nebula winner for Best Novel, Bantam (2009 ER, soon to be in audio by Audible Books 2012)

Tibet series
9. Nothing Sacred—Bantam,1990 (eBook 2010 GSP, soon to be in audio by Audible Books)
10. Last Refuge-Bantam,1991(eBook 2010 GSP, soon to be in audio by Audible Books)

The Songkiller Saga (eBooks 2010 GSP)
11. Phantom Banjo—Bantam,1991
12. Picking the Ballads' Bones—Bantam,1992
13. Strum Again?—Bantam, 1993

Bibliography

The Godmother Series
14. The Godmother—1994 Hardback, 1995 paper, Ace/Berkley (eBook 2009 E-reads)
15.The Godmother's Apprentice—1995 Hardback, Ace, 1996 paper Ace (eBook 2010 GSP)
16. The Godmother's Web—hardback1998 Ace/Berkley, 1999 paper, Ace/Berkley (eBook 2010 GSP)

(stand-alone)
17. Carol For Another Christmas, hardback Nov. 1996 Ace/Berkley, paper 2008 A/B with Penguin Putnam (also as a play by David Brandl and eBook from Ace)

(stand-alone)
18. The Lady in the Loch Ace hardback Dec., 1998, paper Sept. 1999

Prequel to Cleopatra Series anthology (with other authors) 1999
18.5 Past Lives, Present Tense edited by EAS for Ace1999 (eBook Ace/Berkley 2001)
19. Channeling Cleopatra Ace hardback Feb. 2002, paper 2003 (eBook 2010 GSP)
20. Cleopatra 7.2 Ace/Berkley 2003, paper A/B 2004, (eBook 2010 GSP)
21. Cleopatra 7.2 Ace 2004, paper 2005 (eBook 2010 GSP)

22. Spam Vs the Vampire—paper, print on demand 2011, Gypsy Shadow Publishing (also in eBook format)

anthology selection of short stories by EAS
23. Scarborough Fair hardback 2003, Thorndyke Press, (eBook 2009 E-Reads includes 2 story excerpt from E-Reads)

24. Nine Tales O' Cats—Gypsy Shadow Publishing paperback as print on demand and eBook 2011

Stand Alone Novelette
Father Christmas, Spam the Cat's First Christmas— Gypsy Shadow Publishing, 2012, print on demand paper and also eBook format

Anne McCaffrey and Elizabeth Ann Scarborough Collaborations, all still in print and eBooks by original publishers and audio books, various

Powers or Petaybe series
1. Powers That Be, Del Rey, hardback 1993, pb 1994 (also ebook and audio formats)
2. Power Lines, Del Rey, hardback 1994, pb 1995 (also a&e formats)
3. Power Play, Del Rey hardback 1995, pb 1996 (also a&e formats)

Twins of Petaybe series (YA)
4. Changelings—Del Rey hardback 2005, pb 2006 (also e&a formats)
5. Maelstrom—Del Rey 2007 hardback, 2010, Dec. 2010 pb (also e&a formats)
6. Deluge—Del Rey 2009 hardback, 1010 pb (also e&a formats)

Tales of the Barque Cats (YA)
7. Catalyst—Del Rey 2010 hardback, 2011 pb. (also e&a formats)
8. Catacombs—Del Rey 2011, hardback, 2012 paper (also e&a formats)

In the Acorna series. The first two books in this series, Acorna and Acorna's Quest were by Anne McCaffrey and Margaret Ball. I picked up when Acorna returned to her homeworld. I was writing 2 books a year at this point, sometimes in the same year as my solo books, sometimes in the same year as the Twins of Petyabe series with Del Rey. These are all supposed to be for young adults. There is a good cat in this series, for my cat-loving fans)

9. Acorna's People—Harper Collins June 1999, paperback August 2000. (also e&a)
10. Acorna's World—Harper Collins, hard back 2000, paper 2001 (also in a&e formats)
11. Acorna's Search—Harper Collins, hardback Jan. 2002, Paper Dec. 2002 (also in e&a formats)
12. Acorna's Rebels—Harper Collins, hardback Jan 2003, paper Oct. 2003 (also in e&a formats)
13. Acorna's Triumph—EOS (YA division of Harper Collins), hardback 2003, pb 2004 (also in e&a)

ACORNA'S CHILDREN series (YA) (good cat in this series too)
14. First Warning—EOS (Harper Collins) hardback (2005), paper 2006 (also in e&a)
15. Second Wave—EOS (Harper Collins) 2006, paper 2007 (also in e&a)
16. Third Watch—EOS (Harper Collins) 2007, paper 2008 (also in e&a)

Anthology co-edited with Anne McCaffrey:
SPACE OPERA—DAW, published 1996 (with stories by Anne and me, but also extremely memorable ones by Peter Beagle, Gene Wolfe, Megan Lindholm (aka Robin Hobb), Marian Zimmer Bradley, Robin Bailey, Alan Dean Foster, Charles de Lint, Robin McKinley and Michael Scott and others) This was a wonderful book and I don't now where the other stories have been reprinted but a used copy of this (Amazon has one) or reprints of these stories by these authors is well worth having).

+ many many short stories

CPSIA information can be obtained at www.ICGtesting.com
Printed in the USA
BVOW060127080312

284702BV00001B/18/P